I0764368

THE GATEKEEPER

THE GATEKEEPER

A Novel

Tom V. Whatley

SANTA FE

Cover photographh by Carl Condit

Sunstone books may be purchased for educational, business, or sales promotional use. For information please write: Special Markets Department, Sunstone Press, P.O. Box 2321, Santa Fe, New Mexico 87504-2321.

Library of Congress Cataloging-in-Publication Data:

Whatley, Tom V., 1940-
The gatekeeper / by Tom V. Whatley.
p. cm.
ISBN 0-86534-427-2
1. Women—Crimes against—Fiction. 2. City and town life—Fiction.
3. Serial murders—Fiction. 4. Police—Fiction. I. Title.

PS3573.H33G38 2004
813'.54—dc22

2004015446

WWW.SUNSTONEPRESS.COM
SUNSTONE PRESS / POST OFFICE BOX 2321 / SANTA FE, NM 87504-2321 /USA
(505) 988-4418 / *ORDERS ONLY* (800) 243-5644 / FAX (505) 988-1025

For

Austin, Allyson,
Lacie, Jackson, Victoria,
and all the children

A CRY FOR HELP SHATTERS THE SILENCE. ANY PERSON with ears can hear it. There is another kind of cry. It can only be heard by skilled ears finely tuned to unspoken words. I can hear. I can help.

–The Gatekeeper

1

NOT A SINGLE LEAF MOVED. THEN SOME STRANGE insect broke the silence, buzzing sporadically as if trying to stay aloft. It was one of those hot Alabama nights. Everything seemed to be in a muggy wilted state. The temperature had been ninety-eight at mid-day. The night, without a breeze, seemed just as hot. Most people were huddled inside their air-conditioned houses.

Not him. He had something to do.

He had entered the gate without hesitation. He liked it inside. A part of him wanted to stay there. He was fortunate. He could always come and go. He was the gatekeeper. As usual, once inside, he felt relaxed and free. No pressure existed. The only rules were his.

He gently moves the glove down on his left hand so he can glance at his watch. Eleven thirty. That's good, he thinks. He stands in the shadows of a large oak. The house is only about fifty steps away, surrounded by overgrown shrubs. They block most of his view of the house. The last light he could see had been switched off at eleven o'clock.

A flash of light catches his attention and he crouches into the shadows. A car comes slowly down the street and passes by. He doesn't move as he looks about for any sign of life. Fences lined with hedges separate her property from the neighbors. The houses to the left and right had been already dark when he arrived. The entire neighborhood seems quiet now. He is relaxed and ready.

He makes himself wait another hour. It is warm inside the zipped up black wind suit. The gloves and ski mask adds to his discomfort. He forces himself to breathe deep and enjoy the moment.

Remembering how the garden came about is a constant replay in his mind. The waiting provides an excellent time to reflect on it again. He has condensed it into three days for the transformation.

The first day was one filled with the sound of a child crying. The wail rises from a ragged splash of shrubs encircled by a fence. The crying goes on and on. Finally, it grows weaker until it is no more than a whimper. Skilled ears would know the snubbing is from a heart cried out. The child is defeated.

Day two is different. A blessed silence permeates the garden. The sound of the breeze forcing its way through shrubs is welcomed. The buzzing of a bee or singing of a bird stirs the music of the heart. This is the day the garden became a refuge from life.

Day three is the day of redemption. The wooden fence and its rickety gate come down. Neglected shrubs and flowers are pulled up, replaced with beautiful blossoms and a sparkling fountain. A white picket fence with a strong gate is wrapped around them. This is the day the garden moved inside his mind.

Turning from his thoughts, he senses it is time. He leaves his dark shadow and walks to the edge of the house. When he gets to willowy shrubs against the house, he slips along the wall checking each window. The first two are locked. He eases under a high window he assumes is a bathroom and the next one he checks is unlocked. He reaches with both hands to push and the window gives under the pressure. It glides quietly upward. He parts the curtains and looks inside. A bedroom. The room is still. No one is sleeping here. He lifts his weight and slides through the window head first, dragging his legs in after him.

Standing in the dark room, he pauses and listens. A strange smell rushes into his nostrils. Popcorn. Burned popcorn. She has been eating popcorn. The door to the room is open. He takes careful steps and leans his head out to look up and down the hall. A small plug-in nightlight casts a low glow at the end of the hall. Her room. The door is closed.

He moves quietly to the door and stands outside listening. The only noise in the house is the steady drum of the central air conditioner. A gentle grip and twist of the door knob and he eases the door open. He can make out the form of her body beneath the covers. He quietly moves to the bed and looks down at her head protruding from the cover. She is on her side facing away from him.

Slipping the rope from his pocket, he wraps the ends around his hands and is immediately flooded with the sensation that always comes at this moment. It is such a thrill to be able to do something to help. If only he could stay inside indefinitely.

He places one knee on the bed and with a single swift movement forces the rope beneath her head and around her neck. He flips her onto her stomach, crossing the rope in the process. He thrusts a knee to her back while he pulls relentlessly with his strong arms. She hardly makes a sound. A faint gurgling noise was all. He holds her this way until he knows she is dead.

The euphoria he feels is almost more than he can take. He holds his position over her, rope cutting into her neck, until his arms grow tired.

It was then he smelled the whiskey. He had overturned a glass on the night stand. No problem. He looks down at the lifeless woman. Removing the rope, he places it in his pocket. She needed to die, he thinks. It will be better now.

He looks around to make sure he leaves nothing. Satisfied, he retraces his route and leaves through the same window. He pulls it down when outside and scuffs the ground a bit to erase any footprints he might leave. He then heads out into the quiet dark night. It's a ten minute walk to where he parked the car. If anyone sees him, he has all the appearances of a neighborhood resident out for exercise.

He slides into the dark blue ninety-seven Tempo. He had left it parked in the darkest area of a strip mall parking lot. The coin laundry is the only business open and two cars are parked in front of it. They are a good two hundred yards from his car. He cases the area, starts the car, and pulls out onto the street. He doesn't flip on his lights until he is out of the parking lot.

The drive home takes about fifteen minutes. He punches the automatic garage door opener while glancing at his watch. Two o'clock. He pulls inside, closing the door behind him.

When he gets out of the car, he takes a plastic bag from a shelf and strips naked. He places everything including shoes, socks, ski mask, and gloves inside the sack. He walks to the door leading from the garage to the back yard and leaves the sack there. Entering his house through the utility room door, he goes straight to a shower in the hallway and scrubs himself completely. When finished, he slips on cut off jeans and a tee shirt.

Back into the garage, he picks up the plastic sack on his way to the back yard. The yard is very private, lined with a six foot fence and much taller shrubs. He goes to his old grill made from a fifty-five gallon drum and lifts the lid. Placing the sack on the grill surface, he douses the sack with lighter fluid, sets fire to it and continues to squirt the flammable liquid on it as it blazes up. The plastic melts quickly and then the clothes began to burn. He waits a few minutes before closing the lid and venting the grill. Later, he will gather the cold ashes into a bag and place them in the garbage container to be picked up by the sanitation department.

As much as he hates to, it is time to leave. On his way out he goes by the trophy case and places his latest trophy on the shelf.

It is much like all the others. The only difference is the name inscribed on the brass plate at its base. He pauses for a minute and looks at the name. Popcorn. It is a good name and a good memory. He turns and walks away, closing the gate behind him.

2

LANE COLE WAS BOUNCING ALONG ON HIS RIDING lawn mower with his mind a thousand miles from any thought of police work. It was mid-afternoon on Saturday and he was engrossed in his weekly ritual. Brought back to reality by the vibration of the beeper on his belt, Cole kept the mower moving while he pulled the beeper to eye level. The number on the digital screen brought him to a halt and he headed for the porch where he had left his cell phone. He punched in the number.

"Hello," answered Chief Phillip Ross.

"Chief, this is Cole. You trying to get a hold of me?"

"I'm on my way over to one-three-nine-five East Pasadena. We've got a dead woman over there. Meet me as soon as you can. Her kid returned from an overnight camping trip and found her. He called nine-one-one and Officer Pruitt responded. Pruitt said it looked like she'd been strangled."

"Give me about fifteen minutes. Tell Pruitt to make sure he closes off the scene until I get there."

Cole rushed into the house, changed clothes without showering, and jumped into his car. East Pasadena was only about ten minutes from where he lived.

In no time Cole was pulling off the street in front of the address. The fire department emergency response vehicle was there with lights flashing. Two patrol cars and the chief's car, along with the ambulance from Helen Keller Hospital, were scattered in the driveway and along the street.

Cole walked up to Officer Pruitt, a young patrolman who looked a little rattled.

"What you got?"

"A white female, looks to be about forty, dead in her bed. Her boy, name's Billy, is sitting in the living room. He found her. I saw the marks on her throat."

"What's her name?"

"Boy says it's Mary Hartwell."

"Okay. Keep everybody out until I tell you different."

Cole stepped inside and the boy looked up with dazed eyes. Cole walked over to him and put his hand on the lad's shoulder.

"I'm sorry about this son," Cole said softly.

The boy looked up and acknowledged Cole with a nod. Cole then headed down the hall where he found Chief Ross standing outside the victim's room.

"She's in here," Ross said.

Cole stood in the doorway scanning the room. The bed cover was down to the woman's waist. Slipping on his rubber gloves, he walked over to the bedside. He saw nothing indicating a struggle. He could easily make out the rope marks on the woman's neck. The rope had cut into her skin and the bloody abrasion was clearly visible. He saw what appeared to be a depression on the bed and its cover that more than likely was the print of the killer's knee. Moving around the bed to get a better look, he noticed a glass on the floor. He fished a plastic bag from his pocket and placed the glass inside, lifting it with his pen.

Leaning over the bed without touching it, Cole figured she had been dead a while. He called Officer Pruitt. "Find out from the boy if the door was locked when he came home."

Pruitt returned shortly. "He said it was. He used his key on the door lock and dead bolt. Both were locked."

"Check the other doors and windows, but be careful what you touch. I want to know how the killer got in," Cole said.

Cole then moved slowly around the room searching for any evidence of the intruder's presence. He was crouched down by the bed looking closely at the bed spread when Pruitt returned.

"The house has two more doors. Both are locked and dead bolted. All the windows but one are locked. The unlocked one is in the boy's bedroom on the front of the house," Pruitt said.

Cole and the officer headed to the room and examined the window and floor. Cole knelt and scooped up a bit of a dead leaf and slipped it into a plastic bag.

"The killer probably came through there," he said, motioning toward the window. The detective quickly started a tour of the entire house looking for any telltale signs. Nothing seemed out of place. A bottle of Jack Daniels sat on the kitchen counter. A popcorn popper was on the kitchen counter with the stale smell of burned popcorn lingering as he looked it over.

Meanwhile, Cole pulled his cell phone off his belt and punched in a number. "Mark, get Skip over here ASAP. I want him to brush down this place for prints. Call the coroner. Tell him I need a couple of hours and then he can pick up the body. We're going to need an autopsy on this one." Satisfied, Cole hung up and returned to the bedside of the dead woman. Pruitt was standing by. "Get me a couple of officers over here and have them go door to door in the neighborhood asking if anyone heard or saw anything unusual around here over the last couple of days," Cole said.

Pruitt hurried out of the room and Cole pulled out another plastic bag and retrieved a few loose hairs from the bed spread. He was still looking around the room when Officer Skip Pearl arrived carrying a black leather case. Cole went with him to the front bedroom.

"I think that was the entry, but dust every place that might be a possibility," Cole said.

Pearl got busy and Cole walked outside, noticing that the house was shielded from the street by fences, shrubs, and large trees. He made his way to the window he suspected the killer used and stood to one side, studying the ground. There were no visible footprints, but the ground appeared to have been disturbed.

He made a mental note of it and went back inside to talk to the boy.

3

LANE COLE HAD TWENTY-TWO YEARS OF SERVICE with the Muscle Shoals Police Department. The last twelve had been as one of the department's two detectives. Muscle Shoals was a peaceful small city of about sixteen thousand people. It joined the older cities of Tuscumbia and Sheffield on the south side of the Tennessee River. The city of Florence was just north of the river. The four cities were known as the Quad Cities Area and most recently was tabbed the Shoals. Known for its rich agriculture, beautiful shorelines along the river, the birth place of Helen Keller and blues musician W. C. Handy, a thriving music production area and a relaxed lifestyle, the Shoals was a wonderful place to live and raise a family. With no interstates tying it to the east-west and north-south thoroughfares, it had been a well kept secret for a long time.

The Muscle Shoals Police Department, for a small town, was a well trained and equipped department. A total of forty-six officers worked there. Cole enjoyed his work and was good at it. The only part he didn't like was the part he was up to his neck in at the moment. He had a real soft spot for children.

"Billy, how long were you gone before you found your mother?" Cole asked as he sat down by the boy.

"I didn't come home from school yesterday. The last time I saw her was when she dropped me off at school Friday morning."

"Why didn't you come home?"

"I'm in the Scouts. We left right after school for a camping trip. We meet on Thursday nights and we all packed our things then. We were ready to go right after school."

"What about your father?"

"He was killed in a car wreck when I was five years old."

"I'm real sorry about that Billy. How old are you now?"

"I'm twelve."

"I need to ask you some questions about your mother. If you don't feel like answering them right now, we can do it later."

"Now is okay."

Cole could not help but notice that the boy seemed detached. He figured it was shock. There wasn't a tear in sight. "Was your mother dating anybody?"

"I don't know of anybody coming around here. She never mentioned anybody. Maybe while I was at school."

"Did she seem worried or frightened about anything?"

"Mama drank a lot. I don't guess you would call it worry. She just never was happy after daddy died."

"Did she have a job?"

"Nope. We lived on the insurance money from daddy's death and his social security. At least that's what mama said. She was always saying we didn't have money for this or that."

"Did she ever say she had any enemies or talk about anybody who didn't like her?"

"No. She never went anywhere except to the store and things like that. She don't have no real friends."

"Do you have any relatives that live close by?"

No. My grandma and grandpa live in Missouri. That's where we came from when we moved here. They're my daddy's mother and father."

"Here's what I'm going to do. You can't stay here by yourself and we'll have to close the house while we are investigating your mother's death. I'm going to call the Department of Human Resources and get them to send someone over here who works with children. They will find you a temporary place to stay until we can get in touch with your grandparents. Is that okay?"

"Yes sir. But why would somebody kill my mother? I just don't know who would want to do that to her."

"That's what we're going to try and find out. I'll keep in touch with you because there will be some other things we'll need to talk about. The people who come and get you will know how to get in touch with me. My name is Cole. All you will have to do is ask them. If you need me or just want to talk, have them call me."

The boy nodded and they walked out side where Cole punched in the department number and told a secretary to get the people from the Department of Human Resources over right away.

Crime scene tape was up around the house by the time Human Resources arrived. They went inside with Billy while he packed his things.

After they left, Cole leaned back against a patrol car and thought, I've got a dead woman that's definitely a murder victim and the place is as clean as polished glass. This is going to be tough to crack.

When the officers were through dusting the house for prints and the coroner had left with the body, Cole went inside alone and studied the layout again, trying to get a feel for what had happened. The killer had entered through the window in the boy's bedroom. Unless he had a key, that was the only plausible place. Unless he had a key, Cole thought. He made a note of it in his little spiral pad. There was no sign of a struggle. She probably was drunk and either asleep or passed out when the killer came in. He thought, more likely asleep. The killer was a professional.

Wait a minute, he thought. Why do I feel that way? It was a clean crime scene. The killing was obviously well planned and executed. It seemed the only purpose was to kill the woman. He asked himself, why would a professional killer take the life of an obscure woman in Muscle Shoals who never went anywhere but to the store and had no friends or enemies? That was the question he had to answer.

Cole soon left and made it home for a late supper. He didn't tell his wife Sue much about the case. He just mentioned that there had been a murder and he probably would be tied up on it for a few days. He then spent the evening with Sue and nine year old daughter Molly watching television. They were in bed by eleven and up early on Sunday.

After Cole saw his wife and daughter off to church, he went down to his office. It was small and nondescript, serving both Cole and the department's other detective, Ross Sparks. The weekend work force was out on the streets with only the dispatcher and shift captain at headquarters.

Cole settled into his old swivel chair and propped his feet on the desk. He started to make some notes. The heading at the top of the page read, To Do-Hartwell Murder Case. His first entry: check out the life style of the woman. Did she have friends? If so, who are they and what do they know? Did she have enemies? If her son knew what he was talking about, the answer to both questions was no. She could have kept it from the boy. He had to find out for himself.

The second entry related to the professional nature of the killing. Only time would tell if anything had been taken from the house. He would check her prescription drugs, check book, and cash to see if robbery or theft was involved. There was no sign the house had been searched or ransacked by the killer. It couldn't have been a robbery gone bad because there was no sign of resistance at the crime scene. It seemed the sole purpose of the person who entered the house was to kill her and leave. This bothered Cole.

If a person was that cold and calculating, he could do it again. Cole never touted his expertise as a detective. He knew he was good. The thought of a professional killer working his city caused Cole to think, okay big boy. You better be good 'cause I'm coming after you. You have cranked my tractor.

4

FOR OVER THIRTY MINUTES THE GATEKEEPER HAD relaxed in front of the trophy case and remembered each one. Ruby was the first. He reflected on the moment and swelled with pride. It had been an opportunity. Dion's Ruby Baby was blasting away on the small record player. It was playing over and over. She was passed out on the bed, oblivious to everything. It had been so easy. No planning. No risk. Just do it. A million pounds was lifted off his shoulders with one simple act. He enjoyed the memory.

Cutsie was next. He never planned on there being a next. Cutsie left him no choice. He had invaded the Gatekeeper's world with abandon, hurting an innocent friend. He should have known better. Again it had been easy. Cutsie was weak, even if his words were strong. He assumed his work was done, but Cutsie reminded him it never was.

Years later, fourteen to be exact, Slick came on the scene. Slick had caused an urgency to come up within him, making him throw precaution to the wind. He was lucky. Killing a man under the circumstances of Slick's death was a real excitement. He fought the exhilaration of the event and vowed to be more careful if there was another.

And there was. Two years later it was Velvet. She was easy too. Velvet caused a greater need to arise within him than had Slick. Time was of the essence and he had moved quickly. The joy he felt afterwards kept him inside longer than all the rest.

A matter of months later Summer was placed in the trophy case. She was in process when Velvet was added, but the urgency was not so great. So, he waited and chose the right moment. Velvet and Summer, to be so different, were very much alike. Such good memories, the two of them.

Society Lady was next. My how he enjoyed it. She was better than everyone else. She was so poised and credentialed. She was also horrible. It did him so much good to reach into the social elite and excise a true cancer.

Now, Popcorn. Oh Popcorn. If you had only known the tremendous blessing bestowed upon you. You would be alive today. Yet, you didn't know.

He stood admiring his trophies, reliving the thrill and sense of accomplishment. Suddenly tired, he left, closing the gate behind him.

5

LANE COLE FOLLOWED THE STANDARD PROCEDURE for homicides. He called the Colbert County District Attorney and completed the necessary paperwork to have Mary Hartwell's body and accompanying evidence shipped to Montgomery. The state forensics lab was there and did most of the medical exams, autopsies, and tests. The only evidence he had was the hair collected from the victim's bed. He had no idea how long it would take to get the results of the autopsy. There was always a backlog. He would just have to wait his turn.

After lunch on Sunday, Cole went back to the Hartwell residence and slowly worked his way over the crime scene again, making sure he had not overlooked something. He then visited the neighbors to insure that the patrolmen who canvassed the neighborhood the day of the discovery had not missed anyone who could help. He learned nothing new. She was a loner and nothing had happened to arouse suspicion.

Cole was a thorough detective. He took great pride in his job. This case constantly occupied his mind from the beginning. The professional quality of the murder was more of a mystery to him than the killing itself. Such things just didn't happen in Muscle Shoals. Their killings were usually some domestic situation or a drug deal gone bad. The crimes were always solved in short order. The department had one contract killing during his tenure and it had been solved within a week.

He spent about an hour in the house and then went back to his office.

Monday morning began a two week period of nuts and bolts detective work for Cole. He made some calls to Missouri trying to check out Hartwell's past. Nothing of value was discovered. He got a judge to grant a court order allowing him to examine her bank accounts. Monday morning he arrived at her bank early. He found only a checking account and her transactions were of the same type for as far back as three years. There were no unusual deposits or checks issued on the account.

He had jotted down the names of the pharmaceutical drugs in the victim's house and called the pharmacy listed as her provider. The pharmacist gave Cole the number of pills in each prescription the last time it was filled and there were none missing. There were no hard narcotics on her prescription records so the motive could not have been stealing prescription drugs.

Cole knew the possibility existed that she could have stumbled onto some illegal activity in the neighborhood. People were always learning things that could get them killed. He took the time to check the police report records back over the past two years and the neighborhood was clean. He listed the names of the people who lived in a two block circle around her house and ran them through the police data bank. He came up with nothing.

There was a driving force within Lane Cole to solve this crime. It became a personal thing with him. He seldom let a day go by without reviewing his file and personal notes on the investigation. There just had to be something he was missing. If she had no friends or enemies, didn't go anywhere or have anyone over, had no unusual financial dealings, and was not involved in drugs, then why in the world was she killed?

Another nagging question on Cole's mind was why do we have a professional killer in Muscle Shoals? If he came here just to kill her, the likelihood of encountering his work again was minimal. If he lived here, he could certainly do it again. Like a bolt of lightning, the obvious question flashed across Cole's mind. I wonder if he has. Why haven't I covered that base, he thought. He immediately searched their unsolved murder cases but found nothing close to the same MO. He made himself another note to call the investigators in the three adjoining cities and two county sheriff's departments to ask them to do a search of similar unsolved murder cases.

He made the calls the next morning and then waited. Two days later his office was buzzing. The calls started coming in and before the morning was over he had four other unsolved murders in the two county area. He asked if he could borrow their files and within an hour he had all four on his desk. He plowed into them.

The first was handled by the Lauderdale County Sheriff's Department. The victim actually lived in Killen, a small bedroom municipality to Florence. The murder occurred on July 11, 1992. The victim was a thirty-eight year old black male named Earnest Abercrombie. The killing took place in Abercrombie's parked car outside a popular honky-tonk. Cole's interest picked up when he read the investigator's report. Death by strangulation. There was no sign of a struggle. The victim was seated behind the wheel in the front seat and the killer was obviously behind him in the back seat. Abercrombie had spent a couple of hours drinking and left to go home. The autopsy revealed that the victim was very intoxicated at the time of his death. There were no prints or other evidence found to pursue a suspect. To date no one had come forward with any information. The instrument of death was determined to be a very popular nylon rope, a type found around most households. The marks on the victim's neck helped them arrive at that conclusion.

The second report was from the Sheffield Police Department and it outlined the killing of a resident who lived in the River Bluff region of the city. It was an older yet affluent section near the river. The victim's name was Josephine West. West was thirty-six years old. She was killed in her house on November 18, 1994. The report indicated that she had been strangled by a rope. There were no signs of forced entry. No prints or other evidence had been found. There were no witnesses to the crime and no suspect had been determined after days of questioning neighbors, friends, and family members. Her autopsy revealed a large presence of the prescription drug Zanex in her blood.

The third file was on a woman killed in Florence on February 22, 1995. Cole made a note that this case and the previous death of Josephine West were only about three months apart. The victim's name was Gloria Kingman. She was thirty-five years old. The murder took place in her home. Again there were no signs of forced entry and no evidence to lead to a suspect. The autopsy report revealed death was by strangulation and pictures of the rope marks on her neck accompanied the report. Her blood tests revealed a high level of intoxication at the time of her death.

The last file was from the city of Tuscumbia. Clara Whitmore lived in the section of town featuring large colonial houses and tree-lined streets. The entire city is a historical Mecca and she lived in its heart. She had been murdered in her house on December 1, 1998. She was thirty-eight. Death by strangulation. No evidence. No suspect. The autopsy revealed she had been drinking heavily at the time of her death.

Cole pushed himself back from the desk and walked over to a large map of the two counties. He took a grease pencil and marked an X at the locations of the four cases he had just reviewed and then an X for his case in Muscle Shoals. Cole went to his phone and punched in the numbers for his partner's cell phone. Ross Sparks answered.

"You need to come to the office as soon as you can. The Hartwell killing has taken a strange twist. I need your help," Cole said rapidly.

"I'm on my way," he responded.

Cole and Ross Sparks were a team. It was not unusual that Cole had not brought him into the Hartwell murder. Whoever hit on the case first was the guy who worked it. Both were always busy. However, they were never hesitant to call on each other when they needed help.

Cole was musing over the information in his head when Sparks came in.

"What you got?" Sparks asked.

"Ross, we've had five unsolved murders in Colbert and Lauderdale counties over the past eight years. All have essentially the same MO and none have produced a viable suspect. I've been doing this work long enough to know a professional killing when I see one. Mary Hartwell was killed by a professional. I want you to look over my notes and the files on the other four I've borrowed from Lauderdale county, Florence, Sheffield, and Tuscumbia. I feel strongly we have a multiple murderer hanging out in the Shoals. I think I'll approach the Hartwell case from that perspective. If I'm on target, this will be much bigger than a one man show. I'm going to need your help. If you agree, we need to split up and bleed the other investigators of all the information about their individual cases. We might find something I've overlooked or they just may have a gut feeling that would open a door for us."

"Man alive. I was working on a disc player theft from an automobile parked at Southgate Mall and all of a sudden I'm called up to the big league." Sparks smiled and grabbed Cole's notebook and the case files. "You give me a little time and I'll give you my read. If it matches yours, then we are off to the races. This could be the kind of case you dream about solving."

While Sparks busied himself with the files, Cole flipped through his card index and dialed a number for the local FBI office.

"Federal Bureau of Investigation, Florence office," a female receptionist answered.

"This is Detective Lane Cole of the Muscle Shoals Police Department. I'd like to speak to agent Lang please." Cole really didn't enjoy making this call. He found it hard to like the FBI. They had all the resources in the world at their disposal and small towns like Muscle Shoals often found themselves outside the boundaries of their assistance. Maybe he would get lucky this time.

"Just a moment, please," she said.

"Ted Lang," the agent answered.

"This is Lane Cole. How you doing Ted?"

"I'm fine. What can I do for you today?"

"I've got a murder victim here in Muscle Shoal who was killed by a person I choose to believe was a professional. In checking with the neighboring law enforcement departments, I've found four other unsolved murder cases over the past eight years with almost identical MO's. I'd like you to come over and look at what I've got and see what kind of assistance you can give me. I'm almost certain a profiler would help."

"I'd be willing to do that. I trust your investigating expertise and if you say a profiler will help, then I'll get you one. That might take a few days. If it's okay with you, I'll hold off on coming until I can bring one with me."

"That'll be fine and I really appreciate it."

After hanging up, Cole went back to the task of trying to chart a course for his investigation. He had been busy making notes and detailing plans for about an hour when Sparks turned around in his chair.

"Partner, you're absolutely right in my opinion. We've got us a multiple murderer on the low end of the scale and a serial killer at the high end. What do you want me to do to help?" Sparks asked.

"First off, I want you to talk to the investigators at the Lauderdale County Sheriff's Department and Florence Police Department who handled the investigations in their murder cases. I'll take Sheffield and Tuscumbia. Let's bleed them of everything we can about their findings, the people they questioned, any leads that played out, and any hunches or gut feelings they had or still have about their cases. We've got to cover all our bases."

"I'll get right on it."

"Another thing. Let's keep a tight lid on our thoughts about a multiple murderer. Just tell them we're looking at some similarities. We don't want any publicity about this and you never know who'll go talking to the press. For right now, we'll keep it between us. I'm going to brief the Chief on our investigation tomorrow morning and I'll bring him up to speed. From now on, we are going to keep this thing strictly on a need to know basis. Okay?"

"No problem."

6

PHILLIP ROSS WAS A GOOD CHIEF OF POLICE. HE HAD come up through the ranks, preparing himself well by attending college and countless other law enforcement schools. He had the respect of all his police force and especially that of Lane Cole. Cole was one of Chief Ross's prize possessions. He liked the tobacco chewing country-boy detective that put everybody around him at ease with his down-home ways. Ross had observed him on many occasions as he put the rougher element at ease, getting them to spill their guts about some particular case. He knew Cole worked real hard to make people think he was dumb while he wove a web of precise investigative work that usually tied his cases up in a neat package to present to grand jury or jury in a court case. Ross knew Cole was coming to brief him on the Hartwell murder and was waiting for him when he entered.

"How's the Colbert County Flash this morning?" Ross asked, using the kidding term reflecting on Cole's high school football days at Colbert County High School.

"I don't feel too much like a flash, Chief," Cole answered. He placed a stack of files on the Chief's desk and took a seat. "I've got some things to tell you about the Hartwell case and I need your advice on how I should approach this thing." Cole began his story and brought Ross up to date on the other four murders.

"So you think you've got the same person killing five people in the Shoals?"

"Yes sir."

"Man, this thing's getting bigger all the time."

"Let me tell you what my plans are and you jump in anywhere and tell me if you think I should do it differently."

"Shoot."

"Sparks and I have determined to keep a real tight lid on this. Any kind of publicity could hurt our investigation and cause a lot of problems for us in the community. Right now the three of us are the only ones inside."

"I think that's a must. Go ahead."

"I've called Ted Lang of the local FBI office and asked him to come look at what I've got and he's bringing me a profiler."

"That's good. Make sure you explain to them the confidential nature of this. No leaks."

"Yes sir. Sparks and I will divide the other four murder cases and spend some time with their investigators. We want to make sure they found everything that might help us. Once we've done that, hopefully the autopsy report will be back and we'll have that information to go on. Our next step will be to try to place the five victims in a common setting where the killer could have known them. It is quite obvious he simply wanted to kill them. I am going on the assumption that he knew them. There has to be some connection. The profiler could help us here."

"It sounds like you've got a good plan. You'll find it expanding as the investigation goes forward. Just let me know how you're progressing and how I can help you if you need me."

"Thanks Chief. Well, I'd better go get busy." Cole left the office and got himself a fresh chew of Redman Tobacco as he walked down the hall. The tobacco and solving a case were two things he really enjoyed.

7

LANE COLE AND ROSS SPARKS SPENT TWO DAYS scrutinizing the files of the four murders outside Muscle Shoals. The talked extensively with the officers involved in the investigations. The only thing they accomplished was the definite feeling all five murders were committed by the same person. There were no new discoveries or ideas of a suspect.

Cole revisited the Hartwell crime scene once again. He pulled up a chair and sat quietly in the house for over an hour. He allowed his mind the freedom to drift and think. Is there something here I'm overlooking, he asked himself. He simply had no gut feelings to jumpstart an investigation. His thoughts drifted to the woman's checkbook. One constant entry was the Ice House Liquor Store. He would take a picture of her over there and see if she ever talked to anyone. Cole went back to his office and found the autopsy report.

The State Forensics Lab confirmed death by asphyxiation, or in layman's terms strangulation. The photo of the rope marks on the victim's neck indicated a very common half- inch nylon rope. The report also revealed that she was very intoxicated at the time of death. Her stomach contents were basically tuna and popcorn. There was no sign of her being raped or sexually molested. No foreign hairs or tissue were found on her body or beneath her nails. The report basically confirmed what he already knew. It was a clean kill.

He was still reading the report when FBI Agent Ted Lang walked into his office accompanied by a man he introduced as Agent Lester

Qualls. Qualls was a short stocky man who appeared to be in his late fifties.

"Good to meet you," Cole said with an outstretched hand, getting up from his chair. Cole pulled a couple of chairs over and offered them a seat.

"Ted tells me you think you might have a serial killer on your hands," Qualls said.

"I'm afraid we might."

"Well, the agency pays me to be a profiler of serial killers and I've had a lot of experience and a little success. Why don't you show me what you've got."

Cole pulled a stack of files over to the edge of his desk and opened the top one. "I've got the files here on five unsolved murders in our metropolitan area. They have been committed over the last eight years, all in different police jurisdictions. The most recent one was here in my city. I kinda lucked up on the others. It was clear to me whoever killed the woman in my town was a pro. It was an absolutely clean kill. Just as a matter of covering all the bases, I asked the investigators in the other police jurisdictions here in the Shoals to check their unsolved murder cases. I shared the MO of our killer with them and wound up receiving four files that were very similar, if not identical. I would welcome you to take the files, look over them, and tell me what you think. I need all the help I can get."

"I'll be glad to," Qualls said. "I'd like to take them with me overnight and spend a little time with them."

"I don't mind at all. I have no leads. I am just about to start trying to tie any or all of the victims together. I think the answer to who my killer is will be found when I can do that. On the surface, it appears they did not know each other or shared any common friends or acquaintances. The killer is good . He left no calling cards I can find. All five were killed by strangulation and the rope marks on the victims are very similar. We don't have a single print, fiber, or spot of body fluid from which to check DNA."

“Sounds like an interesting case. I’ll take the files and see what I can come up with. I’ll give you a call tomorrow and we’ll get together.”

They shook hands again and the two FBI Agents left. As they walked away, Cole thought, I don’t know if he can see anything in there that I can’t, but it sure won’t make me mad if he does.

8

QUALLS WALKED INTO COLE'S OFFICE AT EXACTLY three o'clock the next afternoon.

"I spent most of the night and this morning with your files. These cases have a different twist to any I've handled and I've been involved in hundreds," Qualls began.

"What do you mean?" Cole asked.

"First, I too think it is very likely that all five murders were committed by the same person. The clean crime scene produces the puzzle. Most serial killers can be classified by the way they leave their victims. The crime scenes are usually divided into the categories labeled as organized or disorganized. The organized crime scene depicts some shock element the killer wishes to make, like a decapitated head on the mantle. It is obvious such a killer takes his time to organize what will be found. It usually becomes his calling card. The disorganized scene is usually one of bloody upside down mayhem. You know. Blood all over the place and no specific placing of the body or body parts. In your cases, I would classify the killer as very careful and well planned. You are definitely dealing with a very intelligent person whose IQ is very high. I'm sure about that."

"Is that unusual?"

"Not in itself. The unusual part of your cases is the absence of any psychopathic tendency or deviate sexual psychosis on the part of the killer. None of the victims were sexually molested, or physically uncovered or disrobed for that matter. There was minimal loss of blood by the victims. It appears all the killer wanted to do was kill his victims and he did it in a sanitized manner."

"What can you tell me about him. I buy the intellectual part. He is good and careful."

"What I'm going to tell you should not be etched in stone. Quite often my thoughts are supported by facts from thousands of case studies. Other times, they are just my feelings at the moment. When and if you catch your killer, I think he will be a white male in his late thirties or early forties. He will be a well known person who carries out a very successful lifestyle. He will be a professional business man of some sort. I strongly feel your killer is himself the victim of some personality disorder. It is highly possible his disorder involves multiple personalities. If so, the personality doing the killing could reside in the same mind and body without inflicting guilt or shame on the personality everyone knows."

"Hold it a minute. You're getting kinda deep on me Qualls," Cole said.

"I guess it is a little deep. The place where I run into more trouble is victim selection. Random selection and targets of opportunity are the usual style of serial killers, even though they might carefully case them after selection. You have already told me that thus far you've not been able to bring your victims together in any common people groups or circle of friends or acquaintances. But listen to this. They all were between thirty-three and thirty-eight years of age. They all were divorcees or widowed, thus single. They all had the primary care role of children. They all were involved in some form of substance abuse evidenced by autopsy. There are a lot of similarities within your group of victims. I suggest your key to finding the killer might be in the mix of similarities somewhere. Where, I don't know. It could be a substance abuse recovery group or some singles group. I encourage you to check those possibilities out. I've already told you I think the killer is a man. The strength it takes to strangle an adult doesn't necessitate a man. I just have a hunch here. I think the killer knew all the victims and something about their schedules.

All the victims were alone when killed and four of the five were at home. The killer had to have some knowledge about their houses and property. I believe your killer lives right here in your area."

Cole seemed to be a bit overwhelmed with all Qualls said, but for the most part the FBI agent said nothing Cole had not already thought about. The profiler was doing more confirming than he realized. But that was Cole's style. Why inform the agent that this back-woods good old boy could do investigative work. Cole edged him on a bit. "I don't mean to be ungrateful, but you are giving me a profile that includes thousands of people."

"I know it. It also excludes thousands."

"Is this all of your profile?"

"No. Here's another hunch. Your killer has received professional help from a psychiatrist at some point in his life. If that's not the case, he perhaps does extensive reading on the subject of mental illness. He has cried out for help either overtly or covertly. I would imagine the former. A knowledge of mental illness will be a high priority for him."

"Anything else?"

"Yes. One last thing. Don't forget you are dealing with an extremely smart man who probably lives in a world that produces no guilt. You may be waiting for a long time if you count on him making a mistake. Accident or fate may produce him for you, but I just don't believe he'll mess up." Qualls smiled with his last pronouncement.

"I may want to talk to you some more as I work through all this."

"Give me a call."

"I really thank you for your time and help," Cole said as he exchanged handshakes with the agent. Qualls then left and Cole sat down to think.

He had made extensive notes while Qualls talked. The one thing standing out as very important was the thought about the killer having a personality disorder. I'll have to get me some help with that, he thought. With pen and pad, he formalized the profiler's remarks and compared them with his existing notes. From both he began to formulate a game plan. Looking at his watch and seeing he was almost late for supper, he snatched up the files and placed them in a briefcase and headed for home.

Cole, his wife Sue, and nine year old daughter Molly lived in an eight-year-old house next to Sue's mother. It sat on a nice lot, larger than most in the city, just off Second Street. Second Street was one of the major thoroughfares in Muscle Shoals. Sue, employed at a local Insurance Agency, was Cole's best friend. They shared everything except police work. Sue wanted no part of it. Molly was a typical only child. She was totally loved and spoiled. Cole's world smoothed out when he was home. This evening was different.

"Why are you so detached, Lane?" Sue asked. "It's the woman's murder that has you so uptight, right?"

"It's a difficult puzzle, honey. I'm not sure I can put the pieces together."

"You usually don't talk about your work. If you need to talk, I'll listen."

"I know you will. There's no need bothering you with all this. It would probably scare you to death if I did. Just give me time to get a handle on this and I'll be more myself."

"I can handle that," Sue said as she ran her fingers through his hair and left the den.

Cole picked up his notebook and rechecked his notes from the FBI agent. He started listing the similarities of the victims and noting the possibilities of tying them together in a common grouping with the killer. He concluded his initial effort would be to visit all the known substance abuse treatment programs and divorce recovery programs that tend to attract a wide variety of singles. He thought, I'll make a list of both and get Ross to help me contact them. I could get lucky and find that some or all of the victims at some point attended the same group. It would be a start.

9

THE SHIFT CHANGE AT HEADQUARTERS FOUND Detectives Cole and Sparks already at work on Monday morning. Sifting through the phone book's yellow pages turned up five different organizations specializing in treatment of substance abusers. There were two Alcoholic Anonymous chapters and a state operated program at the Riverbend Center for Mental Health. Two religious based programs also operated in the area. Sparks agreed to take the AA groups and Cole took the other three.

Cole's interviews at the Mental Health Center, The Shepherd's Staff, and The New Beginning turned up zilch. All the people were willing to cooperate. None had ever seen any of the victims in attendance at their programs and their records revealed no matches with the victim's names. Cole returned to his office near noon and found his partner waiting for him.

"Bingo," Sparks said with a big smile.

"What did you find," Cole asked with mounting excitement?

"I struck pay dirt at the Sheffield AA Chapter. First thing I learned is that they don't keep records and they don't use last names. It's one of those things they do to make people feel comfortable. I should have known. That's where the anonymous comes in. I thought, shoot, I'm wasting my time. I did show the man who heads up the program the victim's pictures. His name is Loyd Jenkins. He's been involved with the chapter for a long time. He recognized three of our victims right off as people who've attended their meetings in the past. Josephine West, Clara Whitmore, and our woman Mary Hartwell were the people he recognized. None attended for a long time. But hey, I've put three of the five in the same setting. Maybe that's a start."

"You bet it is." Cole thought for a minute and then asked, "Do you think you could get this Jenkins fellow to give you the names of any men he knows personally who have been in the program for a long time like he has, or men who have come and gone over the time period the victims attended? We need to run their names through our database just to make sure we don't have some wacko in the bunch. You need to run Jenkins' name too just to make sure."

"I think he'll help. I promised I would keep his assistance confidential and really stressed the importance of our investigation."

"Then get after it. I'm going to the local libraries and check their sections on psychology to see if there are any of our fine citizens checking out those crazy books on a consistent basis. The FBI man said the killer probably was an active reader of psycho material."

Cole checked the Tuscumbia, Sheffield, and Muscle Shoals public libraries and found them to be lacking in psychology resources of a professional nature. His best bet was the Florence Public Library. When he arrived there, he asked for assistance from the assistant manager and she helped him peruse the material. It was substantial. He produced his badge and informed her he was involved in a serious investigation and asked permission to look at the names of the people who checked out the books.

She led him to an office. They took one book at a time and checked the history of who read them. After going through about twenty books, Cole had a number of names. There were a few duplications. He made a special note of them. He got their addresses from the woman's files. Although he told the woman nothing, he swore her to secrecy. He got the distinct impression that the lady was happy for him to leave.

On his way back to the office he let his mind wander to other resources for people reading current psychology material. The library at the University of North Alabama, located in Florence, would be a source. While almost entirely used by students, he made a mental note to check out the faculty. Then his mind hit on the ultimate source for help. As soon as he was in his office, he phoned FBI Agent Qualls.

"Agent Qualls, May I help you?"

"This is Lane Cole from Muscle Shoals, Alabama. How you doing today?"

"I'm fine. How about you?"

"Me too. I need a little help. I thought maybe you could put the entire nation behind my investigation." Cole chuckled a bit and listened to Qualls do the same. "You mentioned the likelihood of my killer being a reader of psychology material. I was wondering if you could determine the most popular psychology journals, news letters, and periodicals for me and then use your clout to check their mailing lists against the ten or so zip codes for our two county area?"

"Man, you're on the job. That's a good idea. I think I can help you. Give me the zip codes and let me see what I can come up with."

Cole spit out the codes and then asked, "Can you fax me the names when you get them?"

"Sure thing. I've got your fax number in my files. Only one thing I ask. You better call me and let me come have my picture taken with you for the newspaper when you solve this thing." Qualls laughed heartily and promised to get him his info as soon as possible.

Cole thanked him and hung up. Sparks came in soon after and shared the names he'd been able to get from Jenkins.

"Run them through the data base. Wait a minute. I've got a few more I need you to include." Cole looked quickly at the names he picked up from the Florence Library and jotted down four. He handed them to Sparks.

Before Sparks could leave, Cole told him about asking the FBI for help on the mailing lists. "When we get the fax, we will have some more names to run. I don't know if we are getting anywhere, but it sure feels good to be doing something."

"I know," Sparks replied. "I was thinking this afternoon that this case has built a fire under you. I don't think I've ever seen you so possessed by a case."

"You're right. I want the killer. This case is so big most people would think we could never solve it. I want to prove we're big enough to handle it."

"Hey, man. You are one of the best investigators anywhere. You don't have nothing to prove."

"Yes I do. I promise you this thing is not going to get buried in the unsolved murder case file."

"For whatever it means, I'm with you. We'll give it our best." Sparks started to leave.

"Ross, the funeral for Mrs. Hartwell is tomorrow morning. I'm going. I want you to go with me. It's at ten o'clock."

"I'll go. See you in the morning."

10

IT HAD BEEN ALMOST THREE WEEKS SINCE MARY Hartwell's body was discovered. The need for an autopsy occupied most of the following week and Cole learned funeral arrangements were delayed because Billy's paternal grandparents, Earl and Gladys Hartwell, had both been ill. They had waited until they could travel. Mary Hartwell had no living relatives except Billy. Earl and Gladys lived in Missouri and it would be the elder couple who would provide a home for Billy.

Cole and Sparks arrived at Morrison's Funeral Home in Tuscumbia around nine-thirty. Sparks sat outside in the unmarked car to watch the people who came to the funeral and to make special notice of anyone who hung outside, drove repeatedly by, or remained in their car during the service. It was a known fact that some killers visited the funeral of their victims. Cole went inside and made his way to the Chapel. Mary Hartwell's body was in an open casket at the front of the Chapel and a few people were standing around it talking quietly. Billy was one of them.

Cole walked down the aisle and put his hand on Billy's shoulder. The lad turned around.

"Hi Billy. How you doing?"

"Hey mister Cole. I'm doing okay."

"I just wanted to come and be with you today," Cole said.

"I'm glad you did. Have you caught whoever killed my mama?"

"No, not yet. But we are working on it."

"I sure hope you do. I want you to meet my grandma and grandpa." Billy walked Cole across the room and introduced him to his grandparents.

"We are glad to meet you Detective Cole. Billy said you were nice to him and we appreciate you looking after his best interest," Gladys Hartwell said as her husband nodded in agreement.

Cole acknowledged their gratitude and assured them of his continued interest in the boy. He then made his way toward the back of the Chapel and took a seat. He glanced at the corpse as he passed by the casket and thought it was amazing how undertakers could take a body in horrible condition and make it look so good.

Cole noticed some name tags on three ladies around the casket with the Hartwell's and confirmed they were from the Department of Human Resources. He assumed they were there out of interest for the boy and their involvement with him. A middle aged couple Cole did not know arrived a little later. They went to Billy and hugged him. After a few minutes of soft conversation they walked back and took a seat immediately in front of Cole. Cole introduced himself.

"I'm Lane Cole, a friend of the family."

The gentleman turned to extend his hand. "I'm Robert Young and this is my wife Sylvia. We took care of the boy for two days right after his mother died."

"That's special," Cole said. He then allowed the man to turn around and he resumed his vigilance of the room.

By the time the funeral began, there was a total of fourteen people in attendance. Three teachers from Billy's school in Muscle Shoals were there along with an assortment of neighbors. Cole remembered them from working the neighborhood shortly after the woman's death.

The minister was a man Cole knew. He had no church and was often called upon when a family needed a minister. He started out reading some scripture and then talked about how he did not know Mary Hartwell. He then went into a lengthy talk about how God takes care of his children and everybody could rest assured she was in heaven. Cole wondered how he could be so sure if he didn't know her. Cole didn't like preachers.

They made him nervous. He always felt like they were slipping up on him with some of those crazy questions. Instead of listening to the continual homily about heaven, he watched the faces and actions of everyone there. He paid close attention to the neighbors.

At the conclusion of the service, Cole left immediately and crawled into the car along side Sparks. They waited and allowed the funeral procession of six cars to pass by. They then dropped into the end of the line and rode to the cemetery. Upon arrival, they stayed in their car and watched as the body was taken and lowered in the grave. There were no unusual people around and Sparks told him none were around the funeral home. They slipped away and headed back to the office.

11

WEDNESDAY MORNING BEGAN A SERIES OF DEAD-END days for Lane Cole and Ross Sparks. They plugged at least fifty names into the data base for felons and did not develop a single person they could zero in on. The AA chapter in Sheffield did not pan out. The three victims had indeed attended the same chapter, but only briefly and over distanced periods of time. They developed no friends or relationships, which is the trademark of AA.

A week after Cole called FBI Agent Qualls, he received a fax containing six names. The six were on the mailing list of at least one major psychology journal or periodical. Cole checked them out and they were all legitimate. The list included the two psychiatrists at the River Bend Mental Health facility and four practicing psychologists in the area. These were people who had a need and did not raise a red flag.

Cole found himself in a seemingly impossible quagmire. He had five victims, living in five different cities, with children in five different schools, families attending five different churches when they went, with absolutely no common point of identity with a person who could have killed them. Was it possible the killer had chosen them at random? While possible, it still did not seem plausible in this case. They went back over every possibility time and time again. Cole reported to the Chief weekly on the status of the investigation and it nearly killed him to have to tell him they were getting nowhere. They had other work to do and were required to busy themselves with the regular cases that seemed so trivial along side the Hartwell case. Whenever possible, they pulled the files out and worked on it. They had promised each other they would not quit.

It was Friday, three weeks after Mary Hartwell's funeral, when Cole went home in the doldrums of hundreds of wasted hours and dead end streets. The last thing he wanted to hear out of Sue was the horrible phrase he heard in her soft voice.

"I'm glad you got home early today. We're going to a church social tonight."

Lane and Sue drove into the upscale subdivision called The Oaks with Lane griping and Sue reminding. Cole went to church with his wife almost every Sunday, but it was with some specific stipulations. They always arrived late because he didn't want to mix and mingle with all the church folks. They always sat on the last pew in the balcony. The balcony was never full, but the last pew was his. One of the reasons he liked it so much was because he could keep his chew during church and replenish it if necessary without anyone seeing him. They always left with the amen and went out the side door. Sue didn't complain. She was proud he was there. Actually, he listened to a lot more than she realized and deep down inside he had strong convictions. It was just a private thing with him. That was exactly why he didn't like getting cornered in one of these church social gatherings. They always got around to church talk.

"I hate these things. I can't believe you've got me traipsing off to one of those sit and chat gatherings with people I don't know," Lane said.

"Lane, forget it. We're almost there and you'll enjoy it. All the other women are coming with their husbands. Besides, I spend a lot of time by myself while you're out solving all the stolen hubcap crimes," Sue replied.

They pulled up to the Nichol's house. About ten cars already filled the drive and lined the street.

"We're not going to have one of those sharing and praying times, are we?" Lane asked as they walked to the house.

"If we do, you don't have to share or pray. Just sit and listen. It'll do you good," Sue said with a victorious smile.

They were ushered in by Julie Nichols. She told Lane the men were out back grilling hamburgers. He headed that way while Julie and Sue went to the den where the other ladies were. Lane ambled over to the group of men and shook hands. He stood and listened to all the small talk, mostly about football and politics. Bill Nichols stood over the smoking grill flipping burgers. When the burgers were done, they followed Bill into the house where they gathered for a blessing and then served their plates.

Lane thought, I sure am lucky. This isn't a serious meeting at all. He chuckled to himself and mused, I could get to liking this kind of church. I wonder if attending this thing means I get Sunday off. No way.

When they finished eating, the group sat and talked. Nothing heavy. Just comfortable talking. Lane was relaxed and a little embarrassed to admit he was enjoying it.

Nancy Foster, seated on the opposite end of the sofa with Lane, leaned out so she could speak around Sue, who was sitting between them. "Lane, I've been meaning to ask you if you ever hear from Billy Hartwell, the boy whose mother was killed?"

"I haven't talked to him since the funeral. I have spoken with the people from Human Resources. They maintain some contact with the family and they say he is doing fine."

"That's so good to hear. I'm the counselor at the school he attended and it broke my heart when I learned of his mother's death, especially the way she died. He had been through so much for a young boy. You know his dad died. Of course you know that. I forget you probably know more about his family than I do."

"Yes, I knew it. I felt bad for him too. He seems like a good kid."

"I had a special place in my heart for him. He was a troubled kid when school started last year. His teachers talked to me about him and I had him come in for a couple of sessions. He had some issues going on in his life that he refused to talk to me about. I assumed they were issues relating to his home life. He demonstrated some definite characteristics of being an abused child."

"Really," Sue said, getting into the conversation. "What did you do to help him?"

"I talked to the Child Welfare division of Human Resources. That's the proper protocol when we suspect child abuse. They have the power to intervene and send the child for counseling without the parent's awareness. Together, we arranged for him to begin seeing Dr. Russell Stevenson, a child psychologist in Florence. Our school system, as well as most of the other systems around, retain him for such cases," Nancy answered, speaking directly to Sue.

A light went on in Lane Cole's head. He remembered the FBI Agent's words, "Someone with a knowledge of or interest in psychology. Russell Stevenson's name was on the fax listing the people who were on the mailing lists for psychology journals. Cole didn't hear Sue say she had heard a lot about Russell Stevenson or Nancy tell how much she respected him. His head was spinning with a cluster of thoughts. I wonder if any of the other children were troubled. Could they have been referred to Stevenson? The children. The connection could be the children.

Cole sat silently, allowing his thoughts to run free. He never noticed the talk dying down and people beginning to leave. He felt Sue's nudge and he realized it was time to go. They said goodbye and walked to the car. When inside, Sue said, "You're quiet. What's wrong?"

"Nothing. I'm just thinking about a couple of things I've got going at the office. Sue, I'm sorry I gave you a tough time about the party. I actually enjoyed it."

Sue looked over at him, reaching over to take his hand, and said, "Thanks. I'm glad you did." Little things meant a lot to Sue. Big things were really special. What her husband had just said was a real big thing. "I love you, Lane Cole."

"I love you too, sweet."

12

COLE WAS IN HIS OFFICE EARLY THE NEXT MORNING. As soon as he arrived he began to formulate a list of the victim's names, the dates of their deaths, the names of their children, and the schools the children were attending when their parents were killed. He was waiting for school to open so someone would be there to answer the phones. Wouldn't it be something if he could tie all the children to Russell Stevenson. This was an angle that never crossed his mind. Well, a little luck is always welcome. He had renewed hope all because Nancy Foster had opened a crack in the door. He was anxious to push the door wide open and see what was inside.

First on his list was Natasha Abercrombie. Her father was killed in April of ninety-two. The Lauderdale County investigator had indicated she was attending Brooks Elementary School at the time of her father's murder. Killen, a small town north-east of Florence, is the home of three Lauderdale County schools, one of which is the elementary school. Cole looked up the number and dialed it.

"Hello. Brooks Elementary. May I help you," a pleasant female voice answered.

"Hello. I'm Lane Cole and I would like to speak with the counselor in your school."

"Do you mean a guidance counselor? If so, we don't have one here."

"I'm looking for the counselor who would help your students with emotional problems. Do you have one?"

"We do not have one on campus. The county system has one and she serves all our schools. Her name is Sylvia Barnes. Her office is at the Board of Education. Let me give you her number."

"Thanks," Cole said as he hung up. He quickly dialed the new number. He was a little shaky. He might be on the verge of linking the victims. Another voice answered and he was connected to Sylvia Barnes.

"Hello. Sylvia Barnes speaking," she spoke.

"Sylvia, this is Lane Cole. I am an investigator with the Muscle Shoals Police Department. I need your help."

"Sure. If I can," she responded.

"I'm doing some work on a murder case here in Muscle Shoals and I'm trying to tie up some loose ends. Because of that, the fact that I called you and the content of our conversation will have to remain confidential. Can you handle the confidentiality?"

"Certainly. I deal with confidential issues all the time. How can I help you?"

"I've been working on some old murder cases and one of them involved the murder of a man who was the father to one of your students. The murder occurred back in nineteen ninety-two. The child attended Brooks Elementary at the time. Her name was Natasha Abercrombie. Were you working for the system then?"

"I certainly was and I remember it well."

"That's great. Did you have occasion to counsel Natasha when her father died?"

"Yes. I remember it well because it was a first for me...murdered parent, you know."

"Did you have occasion to counsel with the student prior to her father's death?"

"How did you know? Somebody's been talking out of turn." She was quiet for a moment. Then continued, "Yes. I saw her on a number of occasions. She had a troubled past. I tried my best to get into it. She was so detached from reality and exhibited all the symptoms of being an abuse victim. She wouldn't let me in, though."

"Then you didn't resolve her problem?"

"No. I did what I could and then consulted with Human Resources and we referred her to our Child Psychologist, Dr. Russell Stevenson. He did wonders for her. Her father was killed before the school year was over. She worked through it and her other issues with Dr. Stevenson. She went on to graduate from high school and is now attending college."

Cole didn't hear a word after the mentioning of referral to Dr. Stevenson. His heart was about to pound out of his chest when he thanked Sylvia and hung up. Oh boy, he thought. Two out of five. This could be my lucky day. No, he chuckled in his thoughts, just good detective work. He looked at his list. Josephine West was next. She was killed in November of 1994. Her daughter's name was Lisa. She was attending Deshler Junior High when her mother was murdered.

Francis King was the Tuscumbia School System counselor and he found her at the central office. After a similar preliminary to his first call, he heard Mrs. King say, "...referred to Dr. Russell Stevenson through the Department of Human Resources."

Three out of five. This thing was getting hotter all the time. Two more calls. Mark Kingsman was the son of Gloria. Gloria was killed just four months after Josephine West. The Kingsman family lived in Florence. Clara Whitmore had lived in the rural part of Colbert County at the time of her death. Her daughter's name was Valarie. Both school system counselors voiced, "Referred to Dr. Russell Stevenson."

"Five out of five. Touchdown," Cole spoke out loud, even though no one was there to hear. He had tied all five victims together with a suspect through their children. Now, what do I do, he thought. I don't have a shred of evidence.

But I do have a name. Russell Stevenson. I'll have more than a name before long. I'm going to know the good doctor better than he knows himself.

13

ROSS SPARKS HAD COME INTO THE OFFICE WHILE Cole was busy checking the various school counselors and had left without knowing what his partner was up to. He was working on an auto theft case. He returned later to find his partner in deep study.

"What got you here so early, pal? The dispatcher said you were here before six o'clock."

"Sit down and let me throw something at you," Cole said with a sheepish grin.

Sparks took his seat and swiveled around to face Cole.

"What would you say if I told you I could tie all the victims of our multiple murder case to one man and he fits the profile the FBI man gave us?"

"I'd say we have ourselves a suspect."

"I feel like we do. I just don't know where to go from here. Let me fill you in."

Cole talked Sparks through his conversation at the party and his series of phone calls. "Dr. Russell Stevenson had the children of all five victims as clients. He's very intelligent, well known, and up to his neck in psychology. I've got the feeling we have lucked up and tied into the killer. The problem is we have no evidence linking him to any of the murders. It's all circumstance. It is not a crime to treat children whose parents are murdered."

"You're right. If we do the normal things we'll tip him off. I mean like getting a court order to round up his records of counseling sessions with the children. We could get a sealed order to tap his phone." Sparks leaned a little closer and whispered, "We could get Patton or one of the other private investigators to do that without a court order." Sparks smiled and winked.

"No. We'll stay within the boundaries with this one. It could be real big. If we don't do it right, we could wind up with nothing." Cole was quiet for a minute. "I want to start by finding out everything I can about Stevenson. For the time being, I don't want anybody in the circle but you and me. At some point along the way we'll bring the chief up to speed."

"I can handle that. What you want me to do?"

"Pinpoint where he lives and locate his office for me. Find out what he drives and get tag numbers. Don't do anything to spook him. I'm going to get busy rounding up some info on this guy's background."

Sparks nodded and left. Cole picked up the phonebook and called the school where Nancy Foster worked.

"Nancy, Lane Cole here."

"Hi Lane. What can I do for you?"

"I need you to help me get a bio on Dr. Stevenson, the Psychologist you referred Billy Hartwell to. I thought maybe the school board had one on file and you might be able to copy it and fax it to me."

"I'll see what I can do. What's this about?"

"I can't tell you Nancy. It is important that you keep this to yourself. I would prefer no one at the board know you copied me his bio. Can you work that?"

"That won't be a problem and I can keep secrets."

"Thanks. I'll owe you one. Do you think you can do it today?"

"It's almost lunch. I'll run over to the board office and see what I can find. If they have it, you will have it too by one o'clock. What's your fax number?"

"It's 383-1112."

"I'll see what I can do."

“Thanks. I’ll be waiting.”

They hung up and Cole looked back over his list of murder victims. He thought, there’s got to be a way I can place this man at one of the murder scenes.

It was a little before one o’clock when a secretary walked into his office with the fax. Dr. Russell Stevenson was born May 15, 1958. That would make him forty-two. Single. No mention of ever being married. He listed no living relatives. His father died when he was two and his mother when he was fourteen. He mentions his paternal grandparents, now deceased, as being the guiding light to his success. He graduated from Millwood High School and did his graduate and post-graduate work at Chicago University. He earned a bachelors degree with a major in psychology, followed by a master’s degree and a PhD in Psychology. His bachelors was granted in 1981. The masters came in 1985 and the PhD in 1988.

He listed employment with the Lifeline Children’s Advocacy Group from 1984 to 1988. He served as a counselor in their program. He moved to the Shoals in 1989 and opened his private practice in Florence. Two references were given and others promised upon request. One was a Dr. Phillip Walters, Dean of the School of Psychological Studies at Chicago University. The other was a woman named Marilyn DeWalt of Chicago. He listed her as a personal reference. Addresses were given for both.

Cole mused over the bio, trying to get a feel for the man who could have killed five people in the Shoals. He thought, if I’m going to get this guy, I’m going to have to get inside his head. I’m not sure I can do that. He opened his notebook and went back over his notes. He began to list things pertinent to the killer with Stevenson in mind. First came the matter of a personality disorder. The FBI man said there was a kind of personality disorder that would allow him to kill and feel no guilt. He made himself another note to talk to some professional in the field. He needed to learn about personality disorders. Next came the statement about the killer’s intelligence. He would need to check his standings in school and talk to his school reference.

Cole knew he was on to something. It felt good to have a solid lead. A plan was taking place in his mind. He would find out everything he could about Stevenson and try to develop a motive. He would try to do it without Stevenson being aware he was a suspect. Perhaps he could put together enough to cause Stevenson to confess when ultimately confronted. If he didn't do his job right, it could blow up in his face. He stood a good chance of having nothing but circumstantial evidence. If so, he would need such strong circumstances that a jury would believe he was the killer without any real evidence.

Sparks returned about mid-afternoon.

"Your man lives at twelve hundred four Shade Street in the Cedars." Sparks flopped into his chair. "He owns two vehicles. A ninety-nine Volvo and a ninety-seven Tempo. His office is on the first floor of the Shafer Building on Tennessee Street. I've got his tag numbers, phone numbers for both home and office, and a Polaroid of his house from the street."

"Good. We've got to do some serious thinking about where we go from here."

"I agree. We could wind up looking like two small town cops if we don't." Sparks' smile didn't hide the serious nature of his statement.

"I want to talk to the chief, but I want this to be more than a few hours old when I do. Let's soak it til tomorrow before we tell him what we've got."

"Suits me."

14

COLE AND SPARKS WERE IN THE OFFICE EARLY THE next morning. Both visited the coffee pot and were cradling their cups and talking the case.

"I can't think of a reason why we shouldn't go ahead and tell the chief about Stevenson. I can think of a couple why we should," Cole said, sipping on his coffee.

"I agree. We are going to need him if we begin any kind of complicated surveillance. We'll have to do some coordinating with the Florence P.D. and he can help us there."

"Yeah. I know. I think we can handle that okay. If we tap his office and home phones, we'll need a judge to grant us a sealed court order. I know the chief can help with it. It will involve the county DA and we may have to involve the Lauderdale County DA and a judge on that side of the river as well. We will also need the FBI to help us with the wire taps. The chief moves in those circles real well and I don't want to try it without him."

"Well, let's fill him in."

Cole and Sparks walked down the hall.

"Chief, we need a little of your time," Cole said.

"Have a seat and help yourself," Chief Ross replied.

When seated, Cole began, "We have a pretty solid lead in the Hartwell murder and the other four cases we've tied to it."

"Great. Tell me what you've got."

"We've got a man we can tie to all five victims. It's weird, but he fits the profile the FBI agent gave us on the murderer." Cole walked the chief through the series of events leading to their discovery of Stevenson. "We don't have a shred of evidence tying him, or anyone else for that matter, to a crime scene. I've just got this feeling that Russell Stevenson is our man."

Sparks nodded and voiced agreement.

"If he's not, then you've got a very rare set of circumstances that would blow the top off an odds maker's scale," the Chief responded. "I'm sure you are aware you are dealing with a very high profile suspect. All heck will break loose if this breaks the news and you don't have anything but suspicion. It's pretty hard to get a murder conviction based on what you think or feel."

"I know it," Cole replied. "I would like to put a tail on the doctor and get a tap on his phones." Cole turned to Sparks, "Let's not forget his cell phone if he has one."

"Got it," Sparks returned.

"Wait just a minute," the chief injected with a strong hint of caution. "They don't just hand out orders for wire taps to everybody that walks through the door. You need to write out a summary of your investigation and reveal how you have arrived at the point of linking your suspect to all five victims. Also tell the avenues you've taken trying to place the victims in a common setting with a single person. Putting them all together with your suspect is a powerful and crucial circumstance. The victims all lived in different cities with no obvious or hidden relationships putting them into any kind of setting with the same person, other that Stevenson. When you have that in writing, I'll go with you to the district attorney and lend my support for the wire taps."

"Thanks Chief. That's exactly what we wanted," Cole said.

"You men know this could turn into a big publicity case. I suggest you keep a tight lid on it. Taking on a highly respected professional person with circumstantial evidence could leave us vulnerable and very embarrassed. There better be no leaks," Chief Ross said emphatically.

"I've been aware of that since his name surfaced. You are the only person outside the two of us who knows. We want to keep it quiet for the very reasons you mentioned. However, the greatest reason we need to keep it quiet is we need the doctor to make a mistake and give us something concrete. If we spook him, we can forget him making a mistake."

"Then let's keep it quiet and you put together your rationale for a wire tap. When you are ready, let me know and we'll start it rolling. By the way. Good work. I knew you would come up with something."

"Thanks Chief."

15

LANE COLE HAD HIS MATERIAL READY FOR THE district attorney by noon the next day. Jack Nance was a good D.A. and had been briefed by Cole earlier in his investigation of the multiple murders. He would be a real asset in getting the wire tap order. Cole called Nance and made an appointment for one o'clock.

Chief Ross, Sparks, and Cole strolled into Nance's office five minutes early and the D.A. directed them to a table where they sat down. He joined them after telling his secretary he didn't want to be disturbed.

"What brings the heart of the Muscle Shoals good guys to the courthouse today?" He wore a pleasant smile belying the hard nosed public defender they knew him to be.

"It's the five murder cases these boys have been working on," Chief Moss said. "Cole has developed a strong lead and we need your help."

"Great. Tell me about it."

"I have a man I can tie to all five victims. His name is Russell Stevenson. He is a child psychologist who is used for troubled children by every school system in Colbert and Lauderdale Counties. When the school counselors have a child they suspect to be a victim of child abuse, they contact the Department of Human Resource. They in turn arrange for Stevenson to see the kid without their parents knowing it. This guy had the children of all five of our victims as clients. He matches to a high degree the FBI profiler's sketch. Take a few minutes and look through this." Cole slid the folder over to him.

They sat quietly while Nance carefully read the report. When finished, he looked up. "Seems to me you've got yourself a suspect. Good work. How can I help?"

"I want to get a sealed court order allowing us to use a tap on his home, office, and cell phones," Cole said. "While we're at it, I would like permission to obtain his phone records without him knowing it."

"This is going to be a little complicated. Your suspect lives in Florence, so we are going to have to work with their D.A. and a judge on that side of the river. I need to tell you I know your suspect personally. He is a respected man in this area and we may run into some trouble getting a judge to grant the court order. Stevenson moves in high circles of social and civic life in the Shoals. We are going to have to be very careful."

"I want to keep this investigation on an absolute need to know basis for that very reason. You are looking at the only three people privileged to the information I've shared with you," Cole said. "If word gets out he's a suspect, we're dead. If we spook him, we'll never get what we want. He's very intelligent and we need him to make a mistake or two. Will you see what you can do for us."

"If he's the killer, then I want him as bad as you do. You bet I'll help."

"What do you suggest?" the Chief asked.

"Let me see if I can get us into see Judge Myers. I think he'll be our best shot. Hold on for a minute." Nance walked over to his desk, picked up the phone and punched in the numbers.

"Ellen, is the judge busy?"

"He's got something at three o'clock and two lawyers are hanging around to see him," she whispered.

"I need to see him bad. Ask him if he can slip out his side door and come to my office. It's important and confidential."

"Hold on a minute," she said as she punched the hold button. About a minute later she came back on, "He's on his way."

"Thanks hon. I owe you."

Nance replaced the phone and walked over to open his door for the Judge. He walked in and shook hands with all four men. He knew them well.

"What's so important you would call me to your office?" Judge Myers said with a smile.

"Take a seat Judge and we'll lay it out for you," Nance said. He handed the report furnished by Cole to the judge and said, "Read this first and then we'll fill in the blanks."

The judge read the report thoroughly, looking up when he came to Stevenson's name. "Uh oh. This is getting interesting." He finished the report and flipped it on the table. "You've picked a big fish. You say in your report you have no evidence from any of the murders tying Stevenson to the crimes. Your only discovery is placing the children of the victims as clients of Stevenson. While interesting and a strong circumstance, it's not much to go on. Your suspect is one of the bright stars in our area. It's hard for me to believe he's your killer. But I've been surprised before. You want me for something more than reading the report. What is it?"

Cole laid out his request.

Judge Myers thought for a moment. "I'll grant the taps for two weeks. That's all. You can have the phone records. They'll be ready in the morning. I must tell you there's not a grand jury that will indict him on what you've got. I wish you luck. I'll coordinate this with Judge Lewis in Lauderdale County so they won't dump on us. I won't reveal the suspect's name if I don't have to. Now excuse me gentlemen, I've got work to do."

Judge Myers walked out and the Muscle Shoals policemen thanked Nance.

"Keep me posted on your progress and let me know if I can help in any other way."

They shook hands and left.

Cole wished for more than two weeks of phone surveillance. He did not push his luck and risk raising the ire of the judge. He got the ball rolling and appealed to the FBI for assistance. To his surprise, they got right on it and had the phone taps working two days later. It could be the multiple murder idea had raised their interest level. With the phone taps in, it was cross your fingers time. All they could do was wait and see.

Cole and Sparks, after a loose consultation with their counterpart in the Florence Police Department revealing no name to them, initiated a careful surveillance of their suspect. It focused primarily on developing a knowledge of his routine. The result was boring. He went to work, returned home, visited a health club for a workout three days a week, and worked in his yard on weekends. He attended the Episcopal Church on Sunday and a couple of civic groups during the week. The man lived a very simple lifestyle. There was no dating or night life. Two weeks of watching him provided a very predictable schedule.

The wire taps gave them less. When they listened to the tapes after the taps were removed, they had absolutely nothing of interest. They had already studied his phone records over the last six months and found no sign of a murderer stalking his prey. It seemed the man was totally dedicated to his work.

"We've got nothing out of this," Cole told Sparks. "This guy gives no indication of another life. There is no trace of a warped mind or sick personality. I keep thinking back to what the FBI profiler told me. Do you think it is possible he's two different people and he never allows anyone to see the bad guy?"

"You know I can't answer that. I don't know one thing about mental illness. You're going to have to talk with someone who knows about those things," Sparks replied.

"That's exactly what I was thinking. Do you remember the name of the goofy guy who talked to us about psychological profiles when we went to the continuing education conference in Nashville?"

"I remember he was from Vanderbilt University."

"I've got a file of the conference here in my desk. Let's see." He opened a folder and pulled out the program. "His name is Dr. Francis Davis. I think I'll give him a call and get an appointment. It's only a little over two hours to Nashville. I could run up there and back in a day."

"Sounds good to me."

Cole got on the phone and set up an appointment in Nashville for one o'clock Monday afternoon.

16

LANE COLE FOLLOWED THE ELDERLY SECRETARY INTO nto the office of Dr. Francis Davis, head of the Department of Psychology, Vanderbilt University. The two men exchanged handshakes and then Davis motioned for the detective to take a chair over to one side of the large office. The professor took a seat across from him.

"What can I do for you?" Davis asked.

Cole took a few minutes to explain the nature of his investigation and then shared the FBI profiler's thoughts about the killer. "The FBI Agent felt the killer could be a person with some form of personality disorder. We've developed a suspect. One of the reasons I came to you is because I could not afford to talk to a professional in our area. Our suspect is a practicing child psychologist. We have five victims over a period of eight years and our suspect is the only person we've been able to tie to all five. He was seeing the children of our victims as clients. All the murders were by strangulation. He used the same type rope in each killing. The crime scenes for all five murders were as clean as an operating room before surgery. We have not one splinter of evidence tying our suspect to any of the cases. I'm searching for answers and I desperately need help in understanding the different types of personality disorders."

"Tell me about the nature of the victims after the killings. Were they brutalized in any way?"

"No. The crime scenes were what we call organized. There was no disarray to the premises or bodies. They were clean kills."

"No messages have been left?"

"None we can find or recognize. No letters or phone calls have been received."

"Do you know the nature of the problems the children were having?"

"No. Well, perhaps. A couple of the school counselors indicated symptoms of child abuse. I would assume that was the case in all five incidents. The children were all taken to our suspect with the assistance of the Department of Human Resources. They are the intervention agency in cases of child abuse in Alabama. The parents were not aware of their children seeing our suspect. I could get a subpoena and go for his records, but that would tip him off. I don't want to do that yet."

"It is obvious that your killer is not a psychopath. The condition of the bodies and crime scene would be quiet different if he was. He is also not a typical serial killer. They usually delight in teasing the police with messages, clues, or repeat behavior. It is almost like a dare to catch them. Sometimes they actually want you to catch them."

"Then what do you think I'm dealing with?"

"First, you must understand that there is a great deal of difference between extreme mental illness and a personality disorder. You have heard references to certain persons having a split personality. What I am talking about is dual personalities in the same individual."

"Is there such a thing?"

"There is a real condition we call multiple personality disorder. Our term is MPD. It really is a rare circumstance. It occurs when an individual develops or exhibits two or more personalities. Each personality within the same individual has its own characteristics, attitudes, and behavior patterns."

"How does a person develop this kind of problem?"

"Our understanding of MPD is still in process. Please understand I am not an expert source for you. I have done extensive reading on the subject and talk to people who study it because it is very interesting to me. The American Psychiatric Association did not consider it as a viable mental illness until 1980. The cases where a diagnosis of MPD have evolved indicate the people went through severe childhood trauma such as physical or sexual abuse. I personally feel this kind of abuse to be the single most important culprit in the formation of the disorder. There are many who believe MPD is caused by a brain abnormality or chemical imbalance. This certainly has been determined to be viable in other forms of mental illness. The truth is, we don't know."

"Put what you've just said in layman's terms for me Doctor. I want to be sure I'm understanding you clearly. I don't run up on this kind of stuff every day."

"Okay. A person can, because of circumstances of abuse they go through while young, actually develop dual personalities. In reality, they are like two distinct people. Changing from one personality to another is usually triggered by some tie to the stress or trauma of their childhood."

"You mean a guy with this MPD can be rolling along in the middle of the day and something can happen that reminds him of the trauma of his childhood and he can flip over to the other person, just like that?" Cole asked with a snap of his finger.

Davis laughed. "I need to remember your description. I could use it in the classroom sometime. But to answer your question, yes."

"Is it possible that one personality could be healthy while another within the same person could be aggressive and dangerous?"

"Quite possible. There was a landmark case in 1979. A Florida woman was found not guilty by reason of insanity in a murder case because the killing took place at the hands of one of eight personalities residing within her body. The primary personality was that of a very congenial, law abiding person."

"Hold it Doc. I'm having a little trouble understanding two personalities. Don't start throwing the number eight around." Cole laughed and shook his head like a kid looking at the nines for the first time in the multiplication tables. "You mean my suspect, if he had MPD, could be a successful and well respected professional in our community while having another personality that could take a person's life?"

"If your suspect truly has MPD, the answer is yes."

"Can you or anyone you know diagnose a person and determine whether or not he has MPD?"

"Diagnosis is very difficult. You would certainly need long periods of time with the person being diagnosed. It could not be done from a distance, such as you telling me about your suspect. You know for certain as an investigator how quick a lot of people rush to an insanity plea as a ruse or escape mechanism. A person with MPD would not recognize it or use it as an escape. There is a lot of work being done with the electroencephalograph. It is an instrument that reads brain waves. There have been some positive results in reading the brain activity of different personalities within a single brain. Having general access to that as a diagnostic tool is a long way off. Diagnosis is just not very easy."

"Okay. Another question. Something happens and the good guy moves over and lets the bad guy take charge. The bad guy kills a person. Does the good guy know what the bad guy has done?"

"There is the good possibility, to use your terms, the good guy knows, but it does not affect him in any way. It's like someone he doesn't know personally lives within his body."

"Man, this is crazy."

"Let's say your suspect was abused as a child. As a result of the abuse, he developed a personality that focused upon it. He came out of his childhood with that personality intact. Your suspect so disciplined the new personality that he kept it subdued while he made it through the rigors of growing up, education, and now the practice of his profession. He is now a respectable individual. However, he embodies the second personality. It is the angry, vengeful, and abused one. He is the person who can be easily triggered to unacceptable behavior. The abused person is your bad guy. He is still very present. What happens when your suspect, the child psychologist or good guy, has a child client who is going through what he experienced himself as a child. It could be the trigger mechanism freeing the other personality, the bad guy, to come to the surface."

"You are saying the good guy could rock along with no problems until a young abused client shows up and whammo, bad guy shows up and solves the kid's problem. Bad guy then leaves and good guy goes right along as if nothing has happened."

"It's possible. It's up to you to determine if your suspect is a MPD victim."

"Could the good guy take a polygraph test with questions about a murder the bad guy committed and pass it?"

"Like a breeze. The good guy has done nothing wrong."

"Tell me Doc. How can I catch the bad guy?"

"You could watch the good guy until the bad guy shows up and catch him in the act of the crime. That could take forever. You could also set a trap and bait him into a shift in personalities. To do that, you would have to know absolutely what the trigger mechanism for the shift is. If I was a betting man, I'd put my money on an abused child. Baiting such a trap could border on being illegal, especially if you get caught." The Doctor winked. "It could also be very dangerous."

"Well, I came looking for help and you've given me enough to keep me busy for a while. I really do appreciate it." Cole thought for a moment. "Tell me something Doc. How did this man wind up a child psychologist?"

"Please don't get me wrong and lump us all in one boat. It is a given in our field that a certain number of us who pursue psychology do so in search of solutions to our own problems."

"Oh. I see where you're going. Like healing yourself?"

"More like understanding yourself."

The two men stood and exchanged handshakes and Cole left. As he drove toward the Shoals, he thought, this thing is getting deeper all the time. I hope I don't drown.

17

LANE COLE WAS BACK IN HIS OFFICE EARLY ON Tuesday, waiting for the chief to show up. Chief Moss arrived right at seven-thirty and Cole went into his office as soon as he settled in.

"Chief, I went up to Nashville yesterday and had a conference with Dr. Francis Davis, the head of the psychology department at Vanderbilt University. He was on the program at the investigation school you sent me and Sparks to. He dealt with psychological profiles in the conference and I felt like he could give me some insight into our suspect in the Hartwell case."

"Did you do any good?"

"Yes and no. He gave me some understanding of the possible personality disorder our suspect could have. He developed a rationale of our suspect where he has a multiple personality disorder as a result of child abuse when he was young. He seemed to think abused children could be the trigger mechanism causing the killer personality to come to the surface in Dr. Stevenson. I don't mind telling you I'm swimming in deep water when it comes to this kind of investigation. I've got this strong feeling Stevenson is my killer. I need your advice and permission for something I want to do."

"What you got in mind?"

"I want to travel to Chicago and nose around a little. I can drive up there and stay a few days cheaper than buying an airline ticket."

"Why do you think going there will help your investigation?"

"I have the name of a neighbor to Stevenson who lived near him when he was a child. I need to find out if there was any indication Stevenson was an abused child. I also want to visit the University where he went to school. I'd like to talk to his major professor while he was in graduate school. I'm looking for anything to give strength to the direction my investigation is headed."

"Lane, I've been proud of your work as a detective. You have always done your best to solve every case assigned to you. You have my permission. How else can I help you?"

"I would appreciate you writing a letter introducing me to the police department up there. I may need their assistance."

"I can do that. When do you plan to leave?"

"Tomorrow morning if it's okay. I don't have anything pressing me here and Sparks has agreed to cover me while I'm away."

"That's fine with me. You can pick up your letter this afternoon. One other thing. You be careful. Chicago is a big town." Chief Moss smiled as he shook Cole's hand.

"I will. Thanks for trusting me on this."

18

COLE LEFT MUSCLE SHOALS AT FIVE O'CLOCK IN THE morning. He spent fourteen hours on the road, stopping only to refuel and grab a sandwich. He arrived in the outskirts of Chicago around seven o'clock, found a cheap motel just off the interstate and checked in. Dead tired, he asked for a six o'clock wakeup call and hit the sack. He was eating the continental breakfast at six-thirty the next morning. When he finished, he returned to his room and checked the telephone numbers for Marilyn DeWalt and Dr. Phillip Walters. He had a number for both he had copied off Stevenson's biographical sheet. He cross checked them with the phone book. DeWalt's matched the one he had and her address was listed as 4214 Windsor. Walter's number was unlisted. He would have to try him at the university.

Cole waited until eight o'clock and dialed DeWalt's number.

"Hello," the sleepy voice answered.

"Hello. Is this Marilyn DeWalt?"

"Yes it is."

"My name is Lane Cole. I'm the special editions editor for the Times-Daily newspaper in Florence, Alabama.. Our paper is doing a special edition on people across our area who impact the lives of children. One of the people we are including is an outstanding child psychologist in Florence whose name is Russell Stevenson. I was looking at a background profile of Dr. Stevenson and found your name as a personal reference. I'm in Chicago on some other business and thought I might give you a call while I'm in town and see if you would be willing to give me a personal interview. I would be happy to meet you somewhere or visit with you in your home."

"Of course I would be happy to. It would be much easier for me if you came to my house."

"That's wonderful. I'm not familiar with Chicago so you will need to tell me how to get there."

DeWalt gave him directions and they set eleven o'clock as the time. Cole left in plenty of time to arrive at her house a little early. He parked on the street and walked up to the door and knocked.

"Hello," Marilyn DeWalt said as she opened her door.

"I'm Lane Cole," he said as he reached to shake her hand.

She invited him in. Cole sat in a chair across from DeWalt and they exchanged small talk as Cole tried to make her comfortable.

"I appreciate you talking to me about Dr. Stevenson," Cole then said as he took out his note pad. "How long have you known him?"

DeWalt, who appeared to be in her sixties, responded, "He lived next door to me and my late husband when he was a child. So I guess you could say I've known him almost all his life."

"You must be special to him to be listed on his resume. Were the two of you very close?"

"He used to come over to our house when he was a kid. My husband took up a lot of time with him when he was home. We never had any children and Bob, my husband, would call him over to our yard and talk. It started that way. After a while, he would come over as soon as he spotted Bob."

"Tell me about his childhood. Did you feel like he would be a successful person as an adult or was it a surprise to you?"

"Oh, he was real smart. Bob used to tell me how quickly he picked up on things he taught him. We both felt like he didn't have much of a chance in life though. His dad died when he was two and his mother was a woman with a lot of problems. To be honest, we felt like Russ didn't have much of a chance." She paused for a moment. A wrinkle of concern creased her forehead. "You're not going to write about this are you? It might be embarrassing to Russ now."

"Of course not. It will only help me to understand the man if I understand how he came to be."

"He used to eat with us a lot. I mean when he was six, seven, and eight years old. We treated him like he was ours. His mother had a drinking problem and kept a steady stream of men coming all the time. Russ would spend a lot of time outside. He never said so, but we believed his mother would send him out of the house. It was heartbreaking. He was a beautiful child. He didn't deserve that kind of treatment."

"Did you know his mother well?"

"Not really. She didn't want to get to know us and we seldom saw her when she was not on the booze."

"Did she seem to mind her son spending time with you?"

"To be perfectly honest, I don't think she knew it most of the time. As long as he was out of her way, she was happy. I would read stories to him and bake him cookies. Bob and I got to where we planned our day to include Russ."

"So, in your opinion, she neglected her son?"

"Off the record, I think she was a no good woman who didn't deserve such a precious child. We often talked about how we wished he was ours."

"Did he ever show any signs that made you think she might be abusing him?"

"Oh, she definitely abused him. Or maybe the word neglect is better."

"I mean physical abuse."

"There were a few times we noticed bruises on his arms and face. He would never talk about how he got them. We would ask and he was smart enough to avoid answering. He was one bright kid." DeWalt paused and thought for a moment. "Mr. Cole, I'm talking way too much. If you write about this, it could hurt that boy all over again."

"I give you my word I will not. You can trust me." Cole could be persuasive when he needed to and he was pouring it on thick.

"I hope so. I would never hurt him."

"I know you wouldn't. Do you remember when his mother died?"

"Certainly. It was a horrible day. I'll never forget the look on Russ's face when we went over to see what was going on. The police and ambulance caused a stir in the neighborhood."

"What kind of look did he have on his face?"

"Well, it was almost like relief. Yes. That's it. Relief. He was fourteen and he had been treated like he was nothing all his life. I'll never forget how he hung onto me and Bob."

"How did his mother die?"

"She was drunk. She passed out and suffocated in her own vomit. They said she was laying face down in her bed."

"Did the boy stay with you during any of that time?"

"No. We would have loved for him to stay with us. They took him away and called his father's parents. He went to live with them and did so until they died. He was in college when they passed away. They were very good for him and gave him a sense of family for the first time in his life. Bob and I felt it was the best thing for him."

"Do you ever get to see him or talk to him now?"

"Not often. He came by about five years ago. Bob died that year and Russ came to see me when he learned about it. We sat for hours and talked about Bob. Russ told me how much he meant to him when he was a child. Russ said he was doing fine and really enjoying his life. He said the great thing about his job was his opportunity to help children."

"He really does help children and it is exactly why we are doing this article. He doesn't know about it, so I would appreciate you not telling him about my visit if he calls you in the next few weeks."

"I won't. Would you mind sending me a couple of copies of the paper when the story is published?"

"I sure will. I will quote you, but it will be a very positive quote and a very positive article. By the way, did the police investigate his mother's death?"

"They did a little. I think they suspected one of her boyfriends might have killed her. In the end, they called it an accident."

"I'm sure it probably was," Cole said as he tried to wind down his conversation. He already had what he needed. He hated to misrepresent himself, but he couldn't afford to disclose his investigation to the woman.

Cole thanked her and left the house. It was almost one o'clock when he got back to his motel. He immediately dialed the switchboard at the university. When he got Walters on the phone, he arranged a meeting in his office for four o'clock. He informed the professor of his real identity and told him he needed some assistance in a murder investigation. After he finished the conversation, he went out to a fast food place and grabbed a burger. He went back to his room and ate while looking over his notes from the visit with DeWalt. He left for the University of Chicago in plenty of time to get there a little early.

"What brings a policeman all the way from Alabama to talk with me?" Walters asked as he offered Cole a chair and took a seat across from him.

"I'm investigating a series of murders in our area and my prime suspect lists you as reference on his resume."

"Who is your suspect?"

"Child psychologist Russell Stevenson. Do you remember him?" Cole checked Walters for any reaction. Stevenson's name got his attention.

"I remember him well," the professor said with a shocked look on his face.

Cole told Walters the need for confidentiality and then explained the circumstances.

"Sounds to me like you have a lot of nothing. It's not a crime for a psychologist to treat children who are legitimate clients. How do you suppose I can help you?"

"I'll admit I'm searching. I'm just trying to understand everything about Dr. Stevenson I can. A FBI profiler told me my suspect could be suffering from some kind of personality disorder. I was hoping you could help me to understand the man and especially help me establish a psychological profile on him."

"I was one of his professors in his under-graduate work and his major professor in his doctrinal studies. I know him well. Ask your questions and I'll try to answer them."

"Did you notice anything about him that would lead you to think he might have a personality disorder?"

"Do you know anything at all about personality disorders?"

"I've spoken with Dr. Francis Davis, head of the department of psychology at Vanderbilt University. He explained the multiple personality syndrome in detail. My question is, did he ever exhibit any behavior causing you to question his stability?"

"First, let me tell you Russell Stevenson is one of the most intelligent students to pass through this university. He was an absolute joy to teach. He gave every indication of being a healthy person." Walters paused in the middle of his conversation and scratched his chin as he thought about Cole's question. "There was one thing that puzzled me a little about him however. It occurred during a low level child psychology class I was teaching in his first year here."

Walters stood and walked over to a large filing cabinet, one of four lining a wall in his office. He opened a drawer, flipped through some files, and pulled out a folder. He thumbed through it for a moment and walked back to Cole holding a typed sheet of paper

"During the class, I asked the students to describe an event or circumstance of their childhood that impacted their lives in some way. Russell wrote this." He handed the sheet to Cole. "At the time I thought he was disclosing an abusive situation of his own childhood. I did not talk to him about it. I decided to observe him closely and see if he carried any heavy baggage from his childhood. I never picked up on any abnormality during years of close association with him."

Cole looked at the paper and began to read.

The Transformation Of My Childhood

The garden was my favorite place. It did not start out that way. As a four year old I was constantly banished to this small area of flowers and shrubs by my mother. It was enclosed by a wooden fence and guarded by a slatted gate. I would be told, "Go to the garden" or "Stay in the garden until I tell you to come out." I hated it then. Mother would force me inside and close the gate. It was lonely inside. It seemed all the fun was outside. The men would come and I could always hear the music and laughter from the house. Often I would curl up in a knot under a large shrub and go to sleep. Other times I would get down on my hands and knees to crawl beneath the shrubs where I could look through the fence. From there I could hear the voices in the house better. I would watch the shadows on the window shades. I could always tell mother's laughter. I wondered why she never laughed that way with me. I only heard it while inside the garden. As I grew older, I got to where I looked forward to the garden. The men would come and I would go there without being told. While inside I could be whatever I wanted to...a pirate sailing the sea or a cowboy riding the range. The garden became the place. While inside, the only rules were mine. I allowed no conflict or hurt there. No one said bad things to me or did bad things to me. I made them stay outside. I became the gate keeper. Mama died when I was fourteen. I had to move away from my garden. It did not matter. The garden had long since ceased to be a physical place. It had become a place in my mind. Through the years of high school and now college, the garden continues to be my favorite place. As the gate keeper, I insure that the mean and ugly remain outside. I alone can enter. Inside, the rules are still mine. I can resolve problems and create change. I can remove pain or fear. I do believe the garden's existence and my ability to go there will facilitate a greater impact upon humanity. Suffering will suffer. The garden transformed my life.

Russell Stevenson

"Kind of interesting. Do you think this could be an indication of some disorder? It sounds kind of kooky to me," Cole said as he looked up from the paper.

"I'm not sure. He had a childhood that produced a capsule of abnormality, evidenced by what you've just read. However, he never evidenced it in any other way."

"I have another question, if you don't mind. According to Stevenson's bio, he was a student here from the fall of nineteen seventy-two until nineteen eighty-eight. He earned three degrees. During that time, do you recall any murders involving students or faculty as victims?"

"We had a faculty member killed in nineteen eighty-two. He was murdered off campus. His body was found in his home."

"Did the police catch the killer?"

"No."

"What was the name of the victim?"

"Edward Prince. He was a philosophy professor. A good one too."

"How was he killed?"

"First, Edward was different. He was an open homosexual. They found him in his den. He had been strangled."

"Did they develop any suspects that you know of?"

"A former lover was questioned extensively and a lot of people thought he was the murderer. The police also questioned a student. He was in a class Edward was teaching and apparently Edward had tried to develop a relationship with the student. The student rebuffed Edward's advances and it was common knowledge. Edward apparently often humiliated the student in class. The student's name was Myron Lesley. He was a weak, skinny sort of guy who had very few social skills. The police thought he had a motive and spent a lot of time trying to implicate him in the murder. Both Lesley and the former lover passed a polygraph test and the police gave up on them as suspects."

"Was Russell Stevenson in that class?"

The professor dropped his head and nodded. "He was the only true friend Lesley had. He stood by him through the entire ordeal."

Cole's head was spinning. Bodies keep showing up, he thought. "Well, Dr. Walters, I appreciate your time. You've been a help. Do you suppose I could have a copy of this paper," he asked?

"I don't see why not." He took it and walked out of the room, returning shortly with the copy.

Cole thanked him and drove back to the motel. It was too late to go to the police department. He would do that first thing in the morning. He needed some time to think anyway.

19

THE NEXT MORNING COLE WALKED INTO THE Chicago police department's seventh precinct and asked to see the commander. He showed his badge to the officer at the reception desk and told him he was on official business. He took a seat to wait. He noticed the commander's name on his office door: Major William Davenport. The officer returned shortly and ushered Cole into Davenport's office.

"Hello, Major," Cole said as he stuck out his hand. "I'm Lane Cole, investigator for the Muscle Shoals Police Department in Alabama."

"Nice to meet you Cole. Have a seat and tell me what in the world you are doing in Chicago."

Cole fished the letter from his chief out of his briefcase. "Read this and it will save us a little time."

Davenport looked it over. "So you're here on an investigation. How does your crime involve Chicago?"

"My suspect grew up and attended college here. He's a child psychologist in our area and my investigation has tied him to five murder victims. I have no evidence, other than circumstantial, involving him in this. I have no witnesses. As we say in Alabama, I'm up here fishing."

Davenport laughed. "Believe me, we fish a lot up here too. How can I help you?"

"I have two old cases in your jurisdiction that I would like to go back and have a look in your department's investigation files. It would help if I could talk to the officers who worked those cases. One involves the death of my suspect's mother and the other the death of a college professor while my suspect was in college. That's why I am here at the seventh precinct."

"Letting you review the records will not be a problem. We'll see what we can do about getting the investigators in here to talk with you."

"That sounds great."

Davenport picked up his phone and punched in some numbers. "I'm sending a Detective Lane Cole from Alabama down there. Assist him in locating a couple of files on old cases and find him a place where he can sit down and review them. He may want to talk to the officers who investigated the cases. Get them in here for him if they're still around." Davenport then placed the phone on the hook and walked Cole to the door. He pointed to the elevator across the lobby. "Go down to the basement and you'll see the records room across from the elevator. The officer's name is Wingate. Let me know if I can be of further assistance. Good luck on your fishing trip."

Cole thanked him and headed to the basement. He found the records room easily and introduced himself to Wingate.

"What records are you interested in?" Wingate asked.

"One is the nineteen eighty-eight unsolved murder case. The victim was Edward Prince, a professor at the University of Chicago. The other is probably a death investigation ruled accidental. The dead person's name was Mary Agnes Stevenson. The death occurred in nineteen seventy-two. I'm not sure of the exact dates."

"Let's give it a try. Follow me."

They walked down rows of filing cabinets and came to one labeled unsolved murders. Wingate opened the top sliding drawer and thumbed quickly through it, looking at dates. He did the same with the second drawer and settled in to scrutinize the third drawer carefully. He straightened up holding three thick folders and placed them on top of the cabinet.

"These are the records for the Prince case. The Stevenson file may be harder to find." Wingate motioned to Cole to follow him as he picked up the folders and walked back toward the front entrance. He placed the folders on a desk in the corner. “Why don’t you get started on these while I look for the other file.”

“Sounds good to me. I really appreciate your help.”

Wingate nodded and walked away. Cole flipped the first folder open and started to read. He took his legal pad and made notes as he went along. He had been at it for about forty minutes when Wingate returned with a single file folder.

“I found the other case. Let me know if I can help you.” He placed the file on the desk and went back to his work. Cole briefly picked up the new file and felt the light weight. Not much in this one, he thought. He jumped back into the file on the Prince murder. After about two hours, he had five pages of notes. He reviewed them.

Prince was found murdered in his upscale suburban house. There had been no sign of forced entry. His corpse was clothed in women’s underwear and pornography was scattered throughout the house. He had been strangled. The impressions left on his neck indicated a common nylon rope. There was no physical evidence found at the crime scene and no witnesses found. An extensive investigation produced no real suspects.

Cole then turned to the investigation of Stevenson’s mother. An autopsy revealed she was extremely intoxicated at the time of death and died from asphyxiation. The conclusion was she had passed out and fell face first onto her large pillow. She had vomited while in that position and it facilitated her death. There was a notation of one detective feeling like her face was pressed too far into the pillow for it to be an accident. Her fourteen year old son was questioned and ruled out as a suspect. A boy friend came in when he learned of her death and volunteered information about being with her the night of her death. He took a polygraph and passed it. With no evidence or witnesses, the case was closed as an accidental death.

Cole thought, this trip has produced two more victims that could have died at the hands of Russell Stevenson. I’ve found no evidence to help me. He looked for the name of the investigator’s in both cases and found a single name. Detective John Smiley. He walked over to Wingate and inquired if Smiley was still on the force. He learned that Smiley had died of cancer three years back.

Cole made a note of the address where Stevenson's body was found. He asked Wingate how to get to there. Wingate produced a city map and pointed out LaSalle and it's proximity to the precinct headquarters.

"That area has changed a lot and it's pretty rough. If you go there alone, you be careful. You'll be the only white person around and you won't be welcomed," Wingate said.

"Thanks," Cole said with a chuckle to himself. Wingate was black.

Cole drove to LaSalle and found the address. The house was in the middle of a row where all the houses looked similar. People were everywhere, sitting on porches and standing in the street. He parked in front of the house, got out, and locked the car. He flipped his badge out so it was clearly visible. He walked into the yard and between the house and a neighboring dwelling. Looking into the back yard, he focused on a grown-up mess of weeds and shrubs surrounded by a decaying wooden fence. His eyes locked on the gate standing half open. His mind drifted to a time when a small boy was placed inside and left alone. He was looking at the breeding ground of a murderer. Having seen enough, he returned to his car and drove back to the motel. He checked out and pointed his car south.

Cole drove through the night, welcoming the long stretches of interstate with little traffic during the dark hours of early morning. It was an opportunity to think. His trip to Chicago was profitable, if not conclusive. He now knew Russell Stevenson was a victim of child abuse. He did not know the extent of it, but could imagine. He also knew, from Stevenson's own written words, that his treatment as a child had been the vehicle of transformation from a real world to an unreal world. It was a kind of spiritual transformation. The man in the garden was no doubt his killer.

He also learned that at least one person felt Stevenson's mother could have been murdered. The suspicion was all Cole needed to confirm the reality. In his heart, he knew Stevenson had done it. The murder of the college professor had Stevenson written all over it. Yet, there was no evidence.

Cole allowed his thoughts to flow. What will I do next? His first move would be to consolidate all the facts and present them to the district attorney and see if he would take the case before a grand jury. It definitely would be circumstantial, but he had a long string of powerful circumstances. People had been found guilty on less, he thought. Then the other half of the equation came forward. A lot of people have been found innocent on more. Well, he would lay it out and see what the D.A. thought.

If the D.A. turns me down, where will I go from there, he asked himself. He remembered what Dr. Davis had told him during his visit to Nashville. He had suggested the possibility of trapping the suspect by baiting him into a situation that would cause him to switch personalities. How could he be trapped? He was way too smart to fall for some trick. But, I could get lucky, he thought. The more sober thought was, I could get into big time trouble.

Cole's business was solving crimes. His jaws were locked on this case like a pit bulldog. There was a plan floating around in his mind. It would be dangerous. Carrying it out would be difficult. The plan became more precise as the sun came up. It might just work. All he would need was the cooperation of the people who would be his players. That might be the hardest part.

20

LANE COLE ARRIVED HOME AROUND EIGHT O'CLOCK in the morning. He and Sue had their time of catching up over coffee. Lane then showered, slept a couple of hours, and left for the office. When he arrived he rounded up Ross Sparks and they went together to the chief's office.

"Was the trip worth it?" Moss asked.

"I confirmed some things and learned some as well. I feel stronger than ever that Stevenson is our killer." Cole walked them through his conversations with Marilyn DeWalt and Dr. Phillip Walters. He drew extensively from his notes and slid his copy of Stevenson's paper across for Moss and Sparks to read as Cole kept talking. "His prof told me there was a murder on campus while Stevenson was a student. He was a philosophy professor who was killed in his home off campus. The murder had the same M.O. as our killings here. They developed no suspects and it's listed as unsolved." Cole filled in the pieces. He then told them about the report on the death of Stevenson's mother. "Of course, again there was no evidence."

Cole did not reveal his thoughts on setting a trap for Stevenson. He would include Sparks later. He would need him. It was premature to do that now.

"I think I'll go to the D.A. with all I've got and see if he will take it to the next grand jury. It would be purely circumstantial. However, if he agrees and we get an indictment, then we could bring Stevenson in and put some heat on him. He might break and confess if we handle it right."

"I don't know, Lane," Moss responded. "The D.A. may not go along with you."

"I've kept him informed about my investigation and he has encouraged me all along. When I tell him what I learned in Chicago, he just might proceed."

Moss replied, "He's good at his work. I know he wants to get the killer. But remember, when this hits the papers, it will be a high profile case. It would stand to make or break him. He has to run for office you know. If he won, he probably wouldn't have to campaign for a long time. If he lost, then he would be back in a law office close to the courthouse like all the other attorneys."

"If the grand jury heard the case, then I could subpoena his counseling records of sessions with the children of the victims. He could have slipped up there. We won't know until we examine them."

"It's worth a shot. See what he says."

"Thanks Chief. Do you want to come along?"

Ross smiled. "No. I'm going to let you do it and if you get yourself out on a limb, I'll deny even knowing you."

They all laughed and the two detectives left the office. Both men knew their chief would support them no matter what happened. Out in the hall, Sparks turned to his partner.

"Lane, this is a big case. It has the potential to get out of hand if any news breaks. We've got to keep it quiet until we're ready."

"I know. I've got something else under my sleeve, but I want to feel the D.A. out first. If he turns us down, then I'll fill you in on my other plan."

"I'm afraid to ask why you didn't mention that to the chief." Sparks smiled broadly.

Cole winked. "If it comes to the back-up, then we might have to do it without the chief's knowledge."

Sparks laughed. "Here we go again. I've always wanted to be a security guard for some used car lot. I can tell you now I already like the back-up plan."

21

COLE AND SPARKS ARRIVED AT DISTRICT ATTORNEY Jack Nance's office at nine the next morning. Cole had filled him in about the nature of the visit when he made the appointment.

"What you got?" Nance asked.

"I want to walk you through the whole investigation and then see if you feel like we've got enough to take it to the grand jury," Cole said.

"Lay it out for me and we'll see."

Cole rehearsed the case against Stevenson from the beginning. Nance listened carefully. The entire process took about an hour. Finally, Cole said, "That's it. What do you think?"

Nance rubbed his face and moved uncomfortably in his chair before he responded. "You've put together a string of powerful circumstances that appear to be persuasive. If I was prosecuting your man, I could certainly make him appear guilty. But I couldn't prove it."

"I know," Cole interrupted. "I'm hoping proceeding to the Grand Jury will allow us to subpoena his counseling records and also give us a shot at interrogating him. He might break."

"Lane, you've got to remember we're dealing with a high profile person. If we jump on this and it backfires, we'll all look real bad."

"It's a risk I'm willing to take."

"Well, I'm not. You know I respect you and your work. You're one of the best anywhere. However, you are neglecting one little thing that falls more under my expertise than yours. This is Colbert County.

More often than not I know the people who sit on a jury in this county. If you are correct in your assumption that the abuse of the children is what triggers your killer into action, we'll have to reveal the nature of that abuse. You stand your suspect up in our courtroom and tell them he's been killing people who abused their children, he'd get a standing ovation. I'm not sure you could find a jury in this county to find him guilty if you had eye witnesses and ironclad proof. Do you understand what I'm saying?"

"So your answer is forget it?" Cole asked, agitation in his voice.

"No. My answer is get me some proof. I'm not going down without it."

Discouraged, but not surprised, Cole thanked Nance for his time and he and Sparks headed back to Muscle Shoals.

Sparks broke the silence. "What are we going to do now?"

"I've got a plan. I don't have it formulated in my mind completely, but I can tell you we're going to move outside the box a little." Cole smiled.

"I figured as much. You can count on me."

"I always know that, buddy. I'm going to get busy on it. We'll have to bring some other people into the plan because we will need more players. I've got to be real careful and make sure they can handle the confidentiality of our investigation. For now, sit on it and let me get my head together."

"Just let me know when you get ready to go. Meanwhile, I've got some work to do on a theft case."

Back in his office, Cole started mapping out his plan. He knew what he wanted to do. If abused children triggered the bad guy to come to the surface, he had to provide Stevenson with an abused child. It would have to be a concocted scenario. Who could he use and who would he need to help? Without much thought, he scribbled the names of Molly...Sue...Nancy Foster...Sparks.

What am I doing, he thought? My daughter in a scheme like this? Molly was exceptionally intelligent and had spent about as much time around adults as she had kids. Her people skills were wonderful. She'd always been dramatic. All of a sudden Cole realized his nine year old daughter could do the job.

Sue was a different problem. She was a good mother and had always insisted on a distance between Lane and his job as far as individual cases were concerned. He would have a hard time convincing her to allow Molly to have a role in his scheme.

Nancy Foster presented another obstacle. He would have to bring a complete outsider into the knowledge and sensitivity of a police investigation. He was certain she would bolt at the first thought of doing so. He would have to approach her carefully.

Sparks was no problem.

He did have one other need, however. There would have to be a house to serve as the residence for his abused child. He remembered a conversation he had with Blaine Jolly, an older retired friend, just a couple of days ago. Jolly had told him that he and his wife were going on an extended vacation to the North West in a few days. He said they would be gone for almost a month. The Jolly's lived in a semi-rural area on the eastern edge of town. The location would be perfect.

22

"NO! ABSOLUTELY NOT." IF LOOKS COULD HURT, LANE Cole would be bleeding. Sue glared across the table, her eyes bouncing with anger. "I can't believe you would think of such a thing, much less that I would agree to it. I've lived with you being a policeman and I've always tried to understand your crazy hours and moods. I even take pride in what you do. But listen, buddy, the job stops with you.

"Hon, just let me explain what I'm trying to do."

"You can explain all you want. There is no way you are going to involve Molly in some farfetched plan to catch a killer."

"I would never think of doing anything to put our daughter in danger. The killer murders people who hurt children. His entire life is involved in helping children."

"Then he couldn't be all that bad. Why don't you leave him alone?"

"He's a murderer and it is my job to catch him. Please let me explain."

"Go ahead, but I'm not changing my mind."

In all their married days, he had never shared his work with her. It felt strange doing so. For the first time she was listening to the details of a murder investigation. To his amazement, she was listening. Somewhere along the way she became interested. He could tell it in her eyes. When he finished, they sat silently a long time.

"Lane, Molly is so innocent. How could you expect her to convince such a man that she's an abused child?"

"Sue, your daughter is smart. She's gifted in this sort of thing. She keeps the both of us convinced about things we know are not true," Lane continued with a smile. "She can carry on a conversation with an adult about anything. She can do it. I know she can. I would work with her. We could both work with her. She would be wearing a concealed mike. I would never be but a few steps away. She would be safe."

"It's easy for you to say, and I believe you. This kind of thing is a normal day for you. You've got to let me think about this a little. I understand where you are in your investigation. I'm just not sure I want Molly to be the bait. She's only nine."

"I hate to remind you sweetheart, but nine year olds are being physically, mentally, and sexually abused every day."

"Let me think about it. I don't want you saying anything to her about it. You understand?"

"Promise. I appreciate you considering it."

Two days later Sue called and asked him to meet her for lunch. They got to the restaurant about the same time and took a table in the back, away from the other patrons. They ordered and talked about their morning until the food came.

As they were finishing, Sue reached over and squeezed Cole's hand. "I've thought about what you said a lot. I appreciate you giving me some time to think."

"Sweetheart, let's forget it. I'll try to find some other way. It's okay. I'm sorry I've stressed you out over this."

"Lane, we've raised Molly to be tough. Let's go for it."

23

COLE'S PLAN WAS RAPIDLY TAKING SHAPE. HE NOW had Molly and he had a house.

The Jolly residence was on Ford Road in the Steenson Hollow section of Muscle Shoals. It was located on a two acre lot with no close neighbors. Perfect. Blaine Jolly had readily agreed. They were close friends and he trusted his pal. "You be sure you don't get my house burned to the ground," had been Jolly's smiling response.

Nancy Foster was a different story. When Cole called to set up an appointment, he asked her the normal procedure for referring children to Stevenson. She informed him that she always made the referral to the Department of Human Resources and their case worker then proceeded in making the appointment if they felt it necessary. That was a wrinkle Cole had not counted on. She gave him the name Kay Moss. Cole quickly asked for Moss to be included.

When they met the following day, Cole filled them in on his plan and walked them through the substance of his investigation.

Nancy Foster spoke first. "Lane, you're trying to get me fired."

"Getting fired is the least of it," Moss said. "I can see myself going to jail."

"I know I'm asking you both to do something with all the appearances of being unethical, Cole said, hoping to calm the conversation.

"Is it unlawful?" Moss asked.

"I represent the law, and I promise you it isn't. You must remember that it is unlawful to murder someone. I know in my heart that Russell Stevenson is guilty of murdering at least five people, possibly seven. And I know he will do it again. This is the only way I can figure to catch him."

"What will we do if your plan fails? My integrity will be on the line and I can tell you the school board will fire me. Kay would certainly loose her job," Foster said.

"If it works, I'll nail him to the wall. If it doesn't, I promise you Stevenson will not pursue any action to get at you. I've got him by the seat of his britches and when I'm finished, his greatest fear will be that it will hit the news." Cole was not as sure of his scenario as he sounded, but he spread it on thick for Nancy Foster and Kay Moss. He needed them.

"I don't like it, but I'll do it," Moss said. "You will have to coach me in what to say and do when the time comes."

"Me too," Foster said with a sigh.

24

"MOLLY, I NEED YOUR HELP," HER FATHER SAID WHEN the family was settled in the den.

"You need my help?" Molly asked, looking over at her mother.

"I'm investigating a case where a woman was murdered. I need someone your age to do a little acting for me." He watched the puzzled look on his daughter's face shift to fear. But just as quickly it was replaced with a smile of excitement.

"I've always wanted to be an actress when I grow up. Do you think this will help me?"

"I don't know about that, but I know you're the one for this job."

Molly looked at her mom again. Her mother smiled and nodded.

"What do you want me to do?" she said, looking directly at her father.

"You know how your mother has always told you to tell her if some adult touched you or spoke to you in a way to make you feel uncomfortable?"

"Yes sir. I know."

"There are a lot of boys and girls who have adults in their lives who hurt them. I'm investigating a case where a mother hurt her son and then someone hurt her. I believe the person who hurt her did so because he was trying to help her son. He was a man the boy was sent to see as a counselor, or doctor. In his, the doctor's, desire to help the boy, he broke the law. It is my job to stop people from breaking the law."

"Daddy, if the man who broke the law was trying to help the little boy, then the law must be bad."

Lane scratched his head and Sue smiled. "Well, we don't make the laws and we don't get to decide which one's are good or bad," he replied.

"What do you want me to.?"

"I want you to go see this counselor and tell him you've been mistreated by an adult."

"That would be telling a lie. Isn't that bad too Daddy?"

"Molly, the man has hurt some people because they mistreated children. It's never right to hurt people. Your father is just trying to stop the man. If we have to play some make-believe to do it, that will be okay," Sue said. "If it works, your father will be able to arrest him and stop him from hurting other people."

"You mean it will be kind of like a movie?" Molly asked.

"Kind of," Lane said. "I want you to go see this man. He's a counselor your school sends children to when they've been mistreated by their parents or some other adult."

"Is he like a doctor?"

"Yes. For children."

"And I will tell him a made up story?"

"That's right. I want you to go see him and act like someone has mistreated you."

"Will he hurt me?"

"Oh no. He loves children. He spends all of his time helping them. It is only adults he hurts."

"He must not be a bad man if he helps children."

"It's the part of him that hurts adults we need to stop."

"What kind of story will I tell him?"

"I plan for you to see him two times. The first time you will not have to tell him much. I will want you to be real sad when you see him and act like you don't want to talk because you are afraid and it hurts you too much to talk about it. The second, I want you to be upset and tell him your mother's boyfriend is coming for the weekend and your mother lets the man touch you and do things to you that you hate."

"What kind of things?" Molly asked, looking at her mother.

"We'll talk about that later. What I want to know is, do you think you can do it?"

"Oh you know I can Daddy," Molly replied with a grin. "I think it will be fun."

"One thing you need to know. It is absolutely our secret. You can tell no one."

"This will be fun," Molly said as she bounced off to her room.

Molly took to the task like a professional. Lane and Sue spent about three hours a night with her. By the weekend she had everything down pat.

25

ON MONDAY MORNING, KAY MOSS PICKED MOLLY up from her father at the Muscle Shoals Police Department. The appointment with Russell Stevenson had been simple to arrange. The small battery powered microphone Molly wore was carefully taped to her stomach. They had tested it thoroughly. Cole explained to Molly he would be close by at all times. If she needed him, he would be there.

Kay and Molly were to be in Stevenson's office at ten o'clock. They arrived ten minutes early. Kay tried to hide her nervousness. Molly was excited.

"Take a seat," the receptionist said. "Doctor Stevenson will be out shortly."

Molly glanced around the room, noticing the bright yellow and blue colors. Pictures of clowns and balloons adorned the walls. Pleasant music was coming from hidden speakers.

Kay Moss patted Molly's hand and whispered, "Relax. Everything will be fine."

At that moment a door opened and a tall, handsome man walked into the room.

"Hello. I'm Dr. Stevenson," he said smiling. "You must be Molly." He walked and took her hand. "Mrs. Moss, relax and make yourself at home. Come with me Molly." Then he led Molly into his office. It was in the same bright colors and there were more pictures of clowns. He offered Molly a chair and quickly sat directly in front of her.

"I'm happy to meet you Molly."

Molly noticed his friendly eyes and thought, he cannot be a bad man. But remembering her role, she didn't respond to his statement. She played the part of a sad little girl like a professional, keeping her eyes on the floor while Stevenson spoke.

"Mrs. Moss tells me your school work has dropped to a level where you are not completing any of your assignments. Your school counselor feels like something is causing you to be sad all the time. They felt it would be good for you to come and talk to me about it. Can you tell me why your school work has changed so much?"

"I don't know," Molly answered in a teary voice. She continued to keep her eyes diverted. "I feel sad all the time."

"Do you know why you feel sad?" Stevenson slid his chair closer and reached over to pat her hand.

"I don't want to talk about it," Molly answered.

"I just want you to know you can talk to me and I won't tell anybody."

Molly looked into Stevenson's eyes. "I don't talk to anybody about how I feel."

"Then let's talk about other things. Tell me the names of your friends."

"Jenny is my best friend. Trey and Susan are good friends too."

"What do you enjoy doing with them?"

"We go to movies, watch TV, and stuff like that."

"Do you know people you don't like?"

"You mean people my age or grown-up people?"

"Both."

"I like most people." Molly seemed to be in deep thought. "There are just two people I don't like."

"Are they children or grown-up?"

"They are grown-up people."

"What about your mother? Is she your friend?"

"I don't want to talk about her," she said, looking down at the floor.

"Okay. Tell me the most fun thing you do."

"Being with my friends."

"What is the least fun thing you do?"

"Going home."

"Why is that?"

"I don't want to talk about it."

"Have you always felt sad?"

"No."

"When did it start?" Stevenson asked, hoping for a different approach.

"Some time after my daddy left."

"Oh, your daddy does not live at home?"

"No. He left. Mama said he didn't want to live with us anymore."

"Is that why you are sad?"

"No. Daddy was never home much. It really didn't bother me much when he left."

"Then why did you start feeling sad after he left?"

"My mother blamed me. She started drinking a lot." Molly straightened up in her chair and looked at Stevenson. "I don't want to talk about that anymore."

"Okay. Tell you what I want you to do for me." He handed Molly a booklet and pencil. "This book is filled with pictures. At the bottom of each page there is a place where you can tell how the picture makes you feel. There are four answers. Each square will have the words very happy, happy, sad, or very sad beside it. Take your pencil and put a check mark inside the square that tells how the picture makes you feel. Will you do that for me?"

"Sure." She took the booklet and started.

When Molly had finished, Stevenson walked her out and asked the receptionist to make her an appointment for next week. Mrs. Moss indicated that Friday at ten o'clock would be the best for her.

Lane Cole had listened to the exchange between his daughter and the killer with sweaty palms. He had been only seventy-five paces from Stevenson's office during the whole conversation.

Molly had handled the situation like a pro. He quickly headed back to his office and was sitting at his desk when the two arrived.

He greeted Molly, hugging her tightly as Kay Moss looked on. "You were great, honey. I knew you could do it."

"It wasn't bad daddy. He's a nice man. Are you sure he's a bad person?"

"That's what we are trying to find out. Were you nervous?"

"Not really. He wants me to come back next Friday," Molly said, not remembering that her father had been listening to the entire conversation.

Cole turned to Kay Moss. "Kay, I thank you for your help."

"I hope it works."

26

ON FRIDAY MORNING, MOLLY AND KAY MOSS LEFT the Muscle Shoals police station a little after nine o'clock. It would put them at Russell Stevenson's office a few minutes before her ten o'clock appointment. Molly was confident. Encouraged by the relative ease of her first appointment and the schooling by her dad and mom over the last week, she felt certain she knew exactly what she would say and do. As Moss pulled into the office parking lot, Molly began to rub her eyes so they would look like she had been crying.

As they walked into the building, Lane Cole pulled into a side street parking place that would allow him a good view of the front door. He adjusted his earphones and took a fresh chew of tobacco. Cole was not a nervous man by nature. He was fighting it now. He crossed his fingers and hoped the bait would be good enough to.

He knew Stevenson was interested. Ross Sparks had tailed Stevenson after Molly's first appointment. He reported that Stevenson had driven by the Jolly residence on Ford Road two different times during the week. Stevenson was all over the bait, Cole thought when he heard the news.

"How are you doing Molly?" Stevenson asked when they were seated in his office. "Have you been crying?"

"I can't stop crying." She began to push tears out and whimper quietly.

"What's making you cry honey? Tell me about it."

"I can't talk about it. He will hurt my mama and me." She began to tremble as she spoke.

"Who will hurt you?"

"It's Don. He's my mama's boyfriend. You sure you won't tell anybody?"

"You can trust me, Molly. I won't tell. Go on now and tell me about Don."

"He lives in Tennessee." she began. "He's been dating mama for a while. He usually comes down on weekends and stays at our house. About three months ago mama left me with him while she went shopping. He grabbed me and held me. He touched me and he made me bleed. I was so scared. When mama came home I told her and she just laughed. She told me she was a lot younger than me the first time that happened to her and I was to keep my mouth shut about it. Don told me he would hurt me and my mama if I told anyone. Since then he does it every time he's here. Sometimes in front of mama. She's always drinking with him when it happens and she just laughs."

"I'm so sorry Molly. You know there are laws that protect you. I can talk to some people and get you out of all this if you want me to. You will have to tell your story to the authorities."

"No! I can't tell anyone. He said he would hurt us if I did."

"I can keep him from hurting you. Your mother would have to go to the authorities to keep him from hurting her. If she told the same story as you, then she may be in trouble with the police."

"I love my mama. I know it's the drinking that makes her like she is. I don't want to do anything to hurt her. She's all I got. I can't tell nobody but you. And you promised."

"I know. But I want you to think about it and let me know if you are willing to tell your story to the police."

"I don't have any time to think about it," she said as tears ran down her cheeks. "Mama's leaving tomorrow morning. She's going to be gone for a week. She asked Don to come stay with me while she's away. I'm so afraid." Tears ran down Molly's cheeks. "Can't you help me?"

A smile broke across Stevenson's face and he cupped Molly's tear stained face in his strong hands. "I can't tell you how, but I promise you Don will not keep you next week."

"How do you know?"

"I just know. I'll keep my promise to you and I won't tell a soul. You just settle down and let me worry about it. When does your mother leave?"

"She said about lunch time tomorrow." Molly wiped her eyes.

"And when is Don coming?"

"Tomorrow morning."

"I want you to go home from school today and be happy. Don will not hurt you again."

Molly jumped into Stevenson's arms and hugged him tightly. "Oh thank you. I didn't think there was anybody who could help me."

Molly wiped her eyes and managed a smile before Stevenson ushered her out to Kay Moss.

"I want an appointment with her next Friday," Stevenson said to Moss.

"That'll be fine," she said as they started for the door. "Same time?"

"Same time."

Lane Cole was beside himself. It could not have gone any better. Molly had been perfect. It seemed that Stevenson had swallowed the bait. All he had to do now was reel him in. I'll have him locked up before tomorrow morning, he thought as he drove toward his office. He glanced at his watch. Almost eleven thirty. He had a lot to do before dark.

27

COLE AND SPARKS WERE INSIDE THE JOLLY RESIDENCE by five o'clock in that afternoon. They adjusted all the curtains and blinds so no one could see inside. They ate their sandwich at the kitchen counter and talked about how they would handle the night. Sue's car was parked in the driveway. They had lugged along Molly's bicycle and left it on the side of the driveway.

Cole would position himself where he could watch the front of the house. Sparks would stay in the darkened kitchen and cover both back entrances.

It had been fairly obvious to them that the killer had walked to the other victim's residences. They assumed Stevenson would do the same tonight. They had to be ready for him at any time. It was their best estimate that he would probably show around bedtime.

By nine o'clock boredom had set in. There was little traffic in front of the house and Cole noticed no movement around the yard. It was a clear night with a half moon.

The wait went on and on. It was now ten thirty and nothing going on. How late will it be before he shows, Cole thought. He's got to come. He promised Molly.

Suddenly, his cell phone vibrated on his hip. He pulled it off the clip and read the caller I.D. It was Sue.

"You need to come home quick Lane."

"You know I can't leave here right now."

"You might as well. Someone just delivered a manila envelope to our front door. It's addressed to you. It's from Russell Stevenson."

"You haven't opened it?"

"Of course not. That's why I called you."

"Well then open it for God's sake."

"Lane, listen to this."

"I will not need to see your daughter again. I am happy to report Molly shows no signs of being an abused child. She does have a very vivid imagination and certainly demonstrates dramatic qualities. Best wishes. Russell Stevenson."

"He knows," Cole said in a whisper.

"What are you going to do?" Sue asked.

Cole thought for a moment.

"I'm going to his place. I'll send Sparks over to stay with you until I get in tonight."

28

WHERE DID I GO WRONG LANE ASKED HIMSELF AS HE raced toward Stevenson's house.

Oblivious to traffic, he soon swerved into the driveway and bolted for the door and rang the bell. He was furious with himself. His suspect had outsmarted him.

Suddenly, he heard the deadbolt shift open. Cole moved squarely in the middle of the door as the strong wooden panel swung open.

"Hello Detective," Stevenson said, stepping to one side. "Won't you come in?"

Stevenson was dressed casually in dark green khakis and a white pull-over shirt.

"Come on back to the den," Stevenson said, closing the door and leading the way.

Cole was surprised to find that Stevenson already had a guest. Dave Hale stood when they walked in.

"Hello Lane," Hale said as he nodded to Cole. "How you doing?"

Cole felt like a boat taking on water when he answered. "I'm doing fine." He tried to hide the cornered feeling emerging in his mind. Dave Hale was a man Cole called friend. It had not always been the case. Cole had watched Hale get a not-guilty verdict from juries more than once when he knew his clients were guilty.

Hale was the best defense attorney in North Alabama as far as Cole was concerned. As a home grown country boy, Hale had achieved his greatness by outworking his adversaries. He had the ability to relate to the people serving on a jury and usually knew many of them personally. Watching him strike prospective participants from the jury was like watching a text book in action.

Hale stood six feet two and his slender frame was accented by long arms, large hands, and long boney fingers. He never overdressed like many lawyers. He could move from the stern look and harsh voice of a country preacher to a calm pleasant demeanor at the flick of an eyelash. He knew the law and he knew all he ever had to do was raise reasonable doubt as to his client's guilt. A witness had better have his seat belt fastened when he took the stand.

His friendship with Hale started when he represented a fellow law officer who was being framed by some local power brokers who could not buy him. Hale ate their sack lunch in court and won Cole's respect. They talked often over lunch since that trial eleven years ago. But Cole knew the friendship thing was out the window when they were working on opposite sides of a case. Hale being here with Stevenson was just another page to a night gone bad.

The trio took seats at Stevenson's insistence and Stevenson broke the ice. "Why do I have the pleasure of your company this evening, Detective?"

"You know why I'm here. You're my suspect in five murder cases. The most recent a lady named Mary Hartwell. She was killed a few weeks back in Muscle Shoals."

"Are you prepared to arrest my client?" Hale asked.

"Not at this time."

"Then Doctor Stevenson has nothing to say," Hale responded.

"I don't mind talking with the detective," Stevenson said. "I know I hired you to look out for my interest. But the detective is just doing his job and he's been wasting his time on me. I'd rather get this settled tonight so he can get on with it. Ask your questions."

"Did you have anything to do with the death of Mary Hartwell?"

"No," Stevenson answered, a relaxed look of innocence on his face.

"Did you know her?"

"No. I had her son as a client. My only knowledge of her was through her son."

"Did you ever visit her house?"

"No. I had no reason to."

Cole mentioned the names of the other victims and asked same questions.

"No," Stevenson answered. "I had a child of each as a client. Of course you know that already and I am sure that is why we are having this discussion."

"You are correct. You are the only person I can bring into the lives of all five victims."

"You mean you've used that circumstance to intervene in this man's life?" Hale asked. "Do you have any evidence to connect my client to your crimes?"

"When I arrest him," Cole shot back, "I'll show you the evidence."

"If your case is circumstantial, I'll make you the laughing stock of the Shoals," Hale said.

"Gentlemen," Stevenson interrupted, "I can tell you he has no evidence because I've done nothing wrong. Now, let's satisfy your mind Detective."

"Would you mind taking a polygraph?"

"There will be no lie detector tests for my client," Hale said adamantly.

"I don't mind," Stevenson said, motioning to his lawyer. "I am honest and can say truthfully I have killed no one. I welcome the opportunity to prove it."

"That's great," Cole said. "I'll get one lined up for you tomorrow morning. I am also going to get a court order to review your files on the children of my victims."

"That won't be necessary," Stevenson replied. "My records are confidential and I could make you get your court order. However, I will have Dave draft a statement making you liable if you disclose the contents of the files. If you are willing to sign it, we can speed up the process. Why don't we meet at my office at ten tomorrow morning. I'll clear my calendar and you can bring your polygraph man. Is that alright with you?"

"That's fine with me," Cole said." I've got one other question. How did you find out about Molly?"

"Before he answers," Hale broke in. "I want you to know the little game you've been playing is the worst case of entrapment I've ever encountered. It could really cost you. If you have damaged this man's good name or ruined his ability to practice in this area, you will be subject to litigation that will own you and everyone else who has touched it. I've already given Russell the name of the best attorney in the state to file the lawsuit."

"There's nothing to worry about," Cole said. "This has been handled in a very tight circle and it will not be broken to the news unless an indictment is issued or an arrest is made. Now back to my question about Molly."

"I knew Molly was not an abused child shortly after she entered my office. Believe me, I know abused children when I see them. I became intrigued as to why she was in my office. I first thought she was playing a game with her parents or the school system. Then the thought occurred that she could be playing a game with me. Soon after she left, I called a private investigator, gave him a digital photo of her, and asked him to check her out. I take digital pictures of all my clients. Unknown to them of course. Before the day was over I knew who she was and had the idea I was being led to some desired conclusion. I then called Dave and told him what had taken place. Entrapment was the descriptive term he used. May I now ask you a question?"

"Go ahead."

"Did you tape my conversations with your daughter? She was wearing a microphone wasn't she?"

"Yes she was," Cole answered.

"I want you to know that Dave was in the next room during the last session. We decided to play along and see where I was being led. Your tape will reveal some interaction with Molly inconsistent with my normal responses to patients. I will allow you to listen to other tapes to prove my point. If my responses to her made you feel I was falling into your trap, that is exactly what I intended. I have an envelope, dated before the last session, sealed and notarized by the probate judge, outlining how I would respond in an attempt to get you to show your hand. You are the one who was trapped."

Cole swallowed hard. "I'm just doing my job."

"I'm willing to help you do your job all I can," Stevenson said.

"Then let's meet tomorrow and get on with it."

Cole was both disappointed and embarrassed as he slid into his car and shut the door. He knew that he had just walked away from a killer. It made him mad that he couldn't prove it. He didn't mind getting his tail whipped. It had happened before and would probably happen again. But he did mind being outsmarted. It's not over, he thought. I'll wait to see what tomorrow brings. In the back of his mind he already knew.

29

COLE GOT BACK HOME AROUND ONE O'CLOCK IN THE morning. He explained briefly what had happened to Sparks and Sue. He got into bed about three o'clock and was up, showered, and at work by seven.

The Chief was already in and had left him a message to come to his office as soon as he arrived. Cole walked down the hall with a cup of coffee in his hand.

"Good morning Lane," Chief Ross said. "I hope you slept well. I didn't. I was on the phone for about an hour early this morning with one Dave Hale."

"So he called and told on me, huh?"

"I told him I didn't know one thing about your crazy scheme and I would make sure you wouldn't have enough ass left to take a decent crap when I got through with you."

"Did he believe you?"

"I don't care whether he did or not. It seems to me you had a good plan for a last ditch effort. I'm sorry it didn't work. I want you to know I'm proud of you for trying and I probably would have done the same thing."

"Thanks Chief. The reason I didn't tell you was because I thought under the circumstances it was better you didn't know. I take full responsibility for it. I don't think we have to worry about liability. The last thing Russell Stevenson wants is public scrutiny of his life. I've kept the lid on this thing very tight. Hale was just trying to scare you into making sure I keep my mouth shut."

"I know it. What are your plans now?"

"I'm meeting with Stevenson and Hale at ten o'clock this morning at Stevenson's office. He has agreed to take a polygraph test. He also has agreed for me to examine the records of his sessions with the children of our victims. He was willing to do that without a court order. I'm going to go over and see how it all pans out. There is the good possibility I'll end the day like I started it. I'll know he is the killer and will have no evidence to prove it."

"Don't get discouraged. Not many men would have found the killer. It could be one of those cases you solve and never prosecute."

"That's what I'm afraid of. I really want him Chief."

"If this doesn't work out, maybe he'll make a mistake later on. I don't think he will stop. Do you?"

"He hasn't yet."

"Well, let me know how your morning goes."

"I will. Thanks again for your support."

Cole and Ross Sparks met the FBI agent who was to give the polygraph test outside Stevenson's office a few minutes before ten and they all went in together. Stevenson and Hale were waiting for them. The receptionist was not on duty. Cole chuckled to himself. He didn't want anybody here, he thought.

"Come on in and we'll get the ground rules set before you begin," Hale said. "Here's the statement you need to sign concerning the files." Hale handed it to Cole. "As for the polygraph, you can ask any benign questions you want to establish a credibility line. After that, all questions will be limited to Dr. Stevenson's involvement in the deaths of the people you claim he murdered. No other questions. You understand?"

"That's not a problem," Cole replied.

"How do you want to proceed?" Hale asked.

"Doctor Stevenson, if you don't mind going into your office with Sparks and the FBI agent, they will get you hooked up and proceed with the polygraph. If I could use this desk, I'll look over the files here. Dave, you can go in with them if you like. It doesn't matter." Cole smiled at his friend. He knew what Hale would do.

Cole then sat down and started looking over the files. He decided to save Billy Hartwell's for last.

For over an hour he studied the files. He held nothing in his hands but printed words. Yet, the voices behind the words cried out from the pages in ear-splitting screams. It was as if he was hearing the children tell their own stories. The tough detective, who had seen more than one person with his head blown half off from a shotgun blast, sat with trembling hands, turning the pages. He couldn't begin to imagine what it had been like for the children. The intrusion upon their bodies. The desecration of their innocence. The raping of their very souls.

Finally, Cole opened the file on Billy Hartwell. He knew this boy. He knew his voice. But the file was intensely more personal. The story of a drunken mother who beat him, locked him in a closet for days, and constantly told him how worthless and unwanted he was. The story of a boy who was always sent off to school with the words, "I don't care if I never see you again." He was the boy who never wanted to dress for physical education because his mother made him wear girls underwear. Everything about Billy's situation made Cole understand why he had triggered the bad guy in Stevenson. The doctor probably saw himself as he listened to Billy.

Cole slowly closed the file and tried to compose himself. The stories of these five children were horrible. How could anyone be so cruel? He now was certain his circumstantial evidence would never get a conviction. He was also certain he didn't want to try. As bad as he wanted Stevenson, he didn't want to waste the case against him with the cards already stacked.

A few minutes later the men came out of Stevenson's office. "This man passed the test with flying colors," the FBI agent said.

"Doctor Stevenson, I want to thank you for your time and apologize for any inconvenience. Again, I am just trying to do a very difficult job."

"I understand Detective. Is there anything else you need from me?"

"No. I don't believe so."

"What about the files? Any questions?"

"No. I think sometimes I have a tough job. I certainly don't envy you. Your job is really tough."

"Yes it is. However, it is a job I enjoy, as I am sure you enjoy yours."

"Yes I do. Thanks again."

"Is this it Lane?" Hale asked.

30

SIX MONTHS HAD PASSED SINCE THE ENCOUNTER with Russell Stevenson. Lane Cole was a bulldog. There was no quit in him. His daily routine now returned to the normalcy of a detective in a small North Alabama town. Shoplifting, auto theft, small home burglary cases, and drug cases were the stuff his schedule was made of.

Never far from it all, however, was a thick file that sat on a shelf above his desk. Not a week went by that he did not take it down and thumb through it. Russell Stevenson was not a forgotten man.

There had been no more killings. Cole and Sparks both took any spare time they could find to keep an eye on Stevenson. Some day he would slip up and make a mistake. Cole had some friends in the Department of Human Resources and they let him know when a child was referred to Stevenson.

On one Friday morning Cole arrived at his desk with the morning paper in hand. He always liked to read it before the place got crowded. A headline caught his attention: "Florence Psychologist To Receive Man Of The Year Award." He quickly read the article. Russell Stevenson was being honored at a noon luncheon held at the Florence Convention Center. I think I'll attend, Cole thought.

The convention center's main ballroom was packed when Cole glanced inside. Since he wasn't invited, he waited outside until the presentation ceremony and then stepped inside to stand along the back wall.

After the award presentation, Cole kept his eye on Stevenson as he shook the hands of a crowd of well wishers. When it was over, Stevenson worked his way toward the main exit. Stevenson extended his hand to the detective when he spotted him in the crowd.

"Congratulations," Cole said.

"Thank you," he replied.

"Are you the gatekeeper?" Cole whispered, as Stevenson started to leave.

Their eyes locked and a chill ran through Cole's body. For a moment he had looked into the eyes of someone who wasn't Russell Stevenson. But suddenly the hard, evil eyes softened and glistened with the moisture of kindness.

"Molly is an exceptional child," Stevenson said in a low voice. "You have been blessed. Be good to her." He then turned and walked away.

Cole realized his palms were sweaty and his heart was beating out of his chest. He breathed deeply and headed for his car.

Sue and Molly looked up with surprise when Lane walked into the den. He never came home during the day.

"What are you doing here?" Sue asked.

"Oh, I thought I might take off this afternoon and try to talk you girls into taking in a matinee and then maybe a pizza afterwards."

31

THE GATEKEEPER HAD BEEN IN HIS TROPHY ROOM for over two hours. He had dusted each one with care. He delicately turned them in his hands. Seven in all. They all held special memories.

When they were back in their special places, he paused and marveled at his work. Satisfaction pulsated through him. But it was tempered by a growing sadness. So many others needed his help. He walked his eyes down the shelf to the last trophy. He then focused on the spot where the next one would rest. Jeremy is such a fine boy, he thought. No child should encounter a predator when he attends church.

Postscript

IT IS NEVER RIGHT FOR A PERSON TO TAKE THE LAW into his own hands. In the instance of abused children, the solution is found in a coalition of parents, counselors, teachers, relatives, government agencies, and precise laws insuring the rights of all children to pass through childhood without abuse.

This book was written to cast light upon the problem. Children are the objects of horrible abuse every day in America. It is dedicated to those who have died or been irreparably damaged because no one heard their inaudible cries. It is dedicated to those in the grip of abuse at this very moment. It is dedicated to those in the trenches–the teachers, case workers, shelter volunteers, psychologists, counselors, advocates for children–people who have developed the skills to hear the children when they don't speak. It is dedicated to tomorrow, hopefully a better day.

The fictional character of Russell Stevenson was himself a victim. His personality disorder is a reality today. There is a part of me that seems to understand him. While his actions are unacceptable, the part of his heart that loved children would have caused him to be my friend.

Outstanding and preeminent Florence attorney Don Holt was used as a character mold for the fictional character Dave Hale. Lanny Coan, successful and respected detective for the Muscle Shoals Police Department served as the character mold for Lane Cole. Both gentlemen are my friends. Nothing in this book reflects how Don Holt practices law or how Lanny Coan conducts himself as a police officer.

www.ingramcontent.com/pod-product-compliance
Lightning Source LLC
Chambersburg PA
CBHW030427310726
48979CB00009B/1656/J
9780865344273